DAPHNE AND VELMA
THE DARK DECEPTION

DAPHNE AND VELMA
THE DARK DECEPTION

BY MORGAN BADEN

SCHOLASTIC INC.

If you purchased this book without a cover, you should be aware that this book is stolen property. It was reported as "unsold and destroyed" to the publisher, and neither the author nor the publisher has received any payment for this "stripped book."

Copyright © 2020 Hanna-Barbera.
SCOOBY-DOO and all related characters and elements
TM & © Hanna-Barbera. (s20)

All rights reserved. Published by Scholastic Inc., *Publishers since 1920*. SCHOLASTIC and associated logos are trademarks and/or registered trademarks of Scholastic Inc.

The publisher does not have any control over and does not assume any responsibility for author or third-party websites or their content.

No part of this publication may be reproduced, stored in a retrieval system, or transmitted in any form or by any means, electronic, mechanical, photocopying, recording, or otherwise, without written permission of the publisher. For information regarding permission, write to Scholastic Inc., Attention: Permissions Department, 557 Broadway, New York, NY 10012.

This book is a work of fiction. Names, characters, places, and incidents are either the product of the author's imagination or are used fictitiously, and any resemblance to actual persons, living or dead, business establishments, events, or locales is entirely coincidental.

ISBN 978-1-338-59273-3
10 9 8 7 6 5 4 3 2 1   20 21 22 23 24
Printed in the U.S.A.   23
First printing 2020
Book design by Katie Fitch

PROLOGUE

The girl has lost count of how many waves she's watched lap the shore. Time has frozen for her. The sun arcs in the bright blue sky overhead. The gulls squawk.

She considers what it would feel like to touch the ocean. To kick the foamy white parts; to dip in a toe. Her feet itch at the chance. Would it feel like a betrayal? she wonders.

It sparkles, this water. The sun continues its slow climb. Its rays make the top of the ocean twinkle, like a billion miniature light bulbs are pulsing underneath the surface. It is her first time seeing the ocean. Her stomach twists and turns at its expanse, at its sheer magnitude. Salt lands on her lips. She misses the desert, the only home she's ever known. She misses the dry air, the sand that would spatter her cheeks on a windy day. But she can't deny the beauty here, and she can't ignore the way the ocean calls to her.

Her mother was right. This place is special. Maybe it'll be the place she can belong.

She pauses; listens. Yes, there it is: From somewhere out on the water, beyond the sound the waves make as they greet the sand, someone is calling her. Or something.

The girl approaches the waves as they rise and fall on the shore. It's not her name she hears—not quite. Instead, it's a faint moan. A whisper. Come to me, *the ocean seems to be saying. Hesitantly, she lets the next wave graze her toes, circle her feet. Then she's ankle deep, her legs trembling from the cold shock of the sea.*

With each receding wave, the girl worries she is losing a part of herself. Under her feet the packed sand is dotted with scraps of seashells. She understands how it feels to be broken like they are—she's been ripped in half herself, part of her still lingering in her old house, her old town, with her old family.

After her parents' split, her mom decided to return to Crystal Cove, the small town on the California coast where she was born. Her dad stayed behind. Now the girl doesn't just miss her old life—she aches with the missing. It's as if the missing itself has become the biggest, most important part of her.

Will Crystal Cove ever feel like home? she wonders as *the water swirls around her, swallowing up her knees. She*

PROLOGUE

researched this town when her parents announced their plans. There's a creepiness factor here; a history that seems to blanket every street corner. Some areas of town have only rickety, leaning old buildings, covered with graffiti and murals of ghosts and monsters. Other parts have sleek condominiums and office buildings, coffee shops and boutiques. Crystal Cove is a study in contradictions.

The girl wades out farther, the ocean now nearly up to her waist. She screws up her face, squints into the sun. She never asked for this. Her eyes well up, but she's not sure if it's from tears or from the sparkling light of the sun, the sea.

Wait. She squints again, brushes away the moisture from her eyes. The ocean has been sparkling and bright all morning, but now? Now, it's on . . . fire.

The girl blinks and takes a step backward. The ocean responds, pulls her in deeper. She kicks her legs, struggles to get back to the shore. She is panting from the effort. As if in surrender, the tide finally releases her from its grip.

On the shore, breathless and sandy and cold, the girl stares. The ocean . . . it's suddenly filled with colors. Bursting up from the foamy tops of the waves are shining bits of red, of green, of blue. It dazzles. Wave after wave creeps up the beach, shining and shimmering in the light. The shoreline is littered with rainbow-colored specks, dots so bright they hurt the girl's eyes.

She scans the beach. It's still early morning, and the rest

of Crystal Cove must still be waking up, brushing off their sleep. She's alone.

She sends a text. **Mom! Something's happening! Come to the beach!**

And then she waits, her back pressed against the empty lifeguard stand, as the ocean spits out its colors, like it's putting on a show just for her.

DAPHNE

"HONESTLY, VELMA, IS THIS really necessary?"

Crouching next to me, Velma Dinkley practically hissed, "Shh!"

I hated to point out the obvious, but I did so anyway. "He's not here yet. We don't have to whisper."

"But he *could* be here any second!" Velma countered.

I rolled my eyes but only a half roll. Because Velma was, as usual, kind of right. Even if she did look ridiculous.

As she nestled even farther down into the narrow space between the back of a bench and the brick wall of the dilapidated Crystal Cove movie theater (now playing: a six-month-old movie that everyone had already seen!), I resisted the urge to take a picture. Velma was dressed in head-to-toe black, including her ever-present combat boots. Even her hair was covered in a black knit beanie cap, and her new glasses—which were, you guessed it, black-rimmed—were slightly too big and covered half her face. She was definitely aiming for incognito but had landed more in the "Wow, is that girl trying to be invisible?" vicinity. Which, knowing Velma the way I do, was an equally plausible possibility.

"What do you think is going on with him?" Velma whispered.

I sighed. We'd had this conversation countless times since the day a few weeks ago that my best friend, Marcy Heller—well, my *other* best friend, since Velma Dinkley had inched her way back into the top tier—had warned me that Shaggy Rogers, one of Crystal Cove High's most popular students, needed our help. What *kind* of help? Well, that was a mystery.

Luckily, Velma and I were pretty good at solving those.

"I honestly can't even imagine what he could need our help with," I confessed. I slunk down next to Velma and rolled my ankles until I heard a satisfying *pop*. Maybe my heeled boots weren't the best choice for today's stakeout. "Shaggy's always been so . . . independent."

Velma chuckled. "Independent. That's a good word for it."

"You would know." I elbowed her. "You're just like him."

"What!" Velma winced when she realized how loudly

she'd gasped. Her voice dropped to a whisper again. "You take that back, Daphne Blake!"

I shrugged. "Hear me out. Shaggy keeps to himself most of the time. He knows everyone, of course, but who really knows him?" Shaggy was easy to be friends with—if you brought him food and petted his Great Dane, Scooby-Doo, he was loyal to you for life—but there was only so much digging under the surface he allowed. He threw parties all the time, which helped cement his popularity at school, but he often disappeared during them, escaping to his bedroom to hang out with Scooby and listen to music. His mother was the chief of police, and his dad—he of the famous Rogers family that helped settle Crystal Cove—had a piece of every business in town. And even though we'd both known him forever, I couldn't think of a single secret of Shaggy's he'd ever revealed to me—not a single worry, or dream, or desire. "Even when we were kids, did you ever feel close to him like you did to me?"

Velma pushed her glasses up the bridge of her nose as she considered this. Years ago, the four of us—me, Velma, Shaggy, and Fred Jones, now a hot member of our school's in-crowd—were super tight. (I guess there were five of us, if you counted Scooby. Which Shaggy definitely did.) We even formed a mystery-solving agency, Mystery Inc., and spent a whole summer finding—and solving— mysteries.

We were ten years old and that was the best summer of our lives . . . until it wasn't. It all fell apart thanks to me . . . but, I reminded myself, things were better now. Much better. Not only had Velma and I made up, but along the way I'd managed to mend my relationship with my mom, and Velma's parents had rightfully regained ownership of their old house and property. Things were looking up for both of us.

"Shaggy *is* hard to get to know," Velma admitted. She trained her serious brown eyes on me, large and intense through her prescription lenses. "And so am I. But don't forget . . . you are, too."

I scoffed. "Everyone in Crystal Cove knows me. And you can thank my mom for that!" Crystal Cove had already had a reputation, thanks to its mysterious history: Three hundred years ago, every resident of Crystal Cove disappeared, save for one. *Poof.* The Vanishing was enough for a town to make its name on, but then Crystal Cove had to go and do something else equally wild: A hundred years later, the entire town burned down. *Poof,* again. Shaggy's great-great-great-whatever-grandfather, Samuel Rogers III, had rebuilt it from scratch. And now here we were: a quiet community on the California coast, surrounded by a sparkling sea on one side and snowcapped mountains on the other, with a history that hung in the air like an impending rainstorm.

DAPHNE

Who knows what the world would think about Crystal Cove today if my mom hadn't gone and designed a video game about it? Every kid who knew anything about gaming—and many who didn't!—had at least heard about *The Curse of Crystal Cove*. Which meant my mom was practically a celebrity. And, in this town, so was I.

"Being popular isn't the same as being known," Velma countered. "And besides, I have a feeling you'd be popular even if your mom hadn't created that game. You've just got that air about you. You know, that *thing*."

I cast my eyes around while I thought about what Velma said. It was true that meeting people and getting them to like me had always been easy. I smoothed my long hair, being pretty had always been easy for me, too. It was funny how, for lots of kids, that was enough to grant me the power of popularity. I'd long ago learned it didn't really matter what I was like inside. I had the smile, the clothes, and the prestige to get whatever I wanted. So, for a long time, I did. I'd decided recently, though, that maybe it was time to show more of me. The real parts.

I was so lost in thought that I almost didn't notice what was starting to happen right in front of us.

Velma and I were on our first official stakeout since we'd sort of, kind of, basically reinstituted Mystery Inc. It was early Saturday morning—early to me, anyway—and one of those sharp fall days where the sun and wind bite against your skin. We were in downtown Crystal Cove, a broad, tree-lined street dotted with stores and restaurants, capped by a large public park on one end and the beach on the other. Traffic was light; just a few people wandered up and down the street or sipped steaming cups on the benches outside my favorite coffee shop, The Mocha.

As I surveyed the scene, I noticed a woman peering into the windows of the toy store. Suddenly, she checked her phone, gasped, and sped in the opposite direction.

"How did we know Shaggy would be here, again?" I wondered aloud, absentmindedly watching the woman from the toy store hurry down toward the beach.

"I tricked him into telling me!" Velma said. Her gleeful tone was muffled from the binoculars—yes, she'd brought binoculars—resting against her face. "I ran into him in the hallway after lunch and asked if he wanted to get coffee this morning, and he said he would be, and I quote, 'like, doing some stuff or whatever downtown.'"

"Hmm."

"I mean, I know I'm no hotshot reporter, but even I can manipulate people into telling me things sometimes," Velma said. She winked at me, but the overall effect was ruined by her glasses sliding down her face again.

"Have you ever considered contacts?" I pushed them up for her—she was still gripping those binoculars—and made

DAPHNE

a face. "And I'm not a hotshot reporter. Just an intern."

"The only junior to ever be chosen for the coveted *Howler* internship, you mean?" Velma nodded approvingly. "Seriously cool, Daph. I've always known you were super smart. I just didn't know you wanted to write. I love it!"

I concentrated on scratching a spot of something— probably dried food from one of my little sisters—on the knee of my jeans and tried to keep my expression neutral. Writing was special to me. Sacred. So sacred, in fact, that almost no one knew I did it—all the time, filling up journal after journal. The Daphne Blake who was known to Crystal Cove High School had a certain reputation already, and being a brainy journalist was not part of it. But regardless, applying for the *Crystal Cove Howler* high school internship had been something I'd hoped to do next year, as a senior.

While the *Howler* itself was mostly a gossip rag, it was the only journalism internship in town. And it did have one section that rivaled the big-city papers: the editorial pages, which ran well-written opinions from important people all throughout California. Scoring their coveted internship was a guaranteed way to make college journalism programs notice you. And Mr. Grimm, my English teacher, had convinced me to apply last month, as a junior, and . . . well, I'd just completed my first week there. And it. Was. Awesome.

11

And not just because of Ram.

Now I was *definitely* blushing. Ramsay Hansen was the other *Howler* intern. But, unlike little old high school me, he was a college freshman, a journalism major at Hartwood University just a few miles away. It was his second semester interning at the *Howler*, which meant that he'd been assigned the task of showing me the ropes. And he did even that with aplomb! In fact, everything Ram did, he did with style. From his clothes—he wasn't trendy in the way I was; it was more like he had a signature look that he'd managed to perfect in his nineteen years—to his work, which even Milford Jones (the owner and editor in chief of the *Howler*) complimented, to his writing, Ram had his stuff together.

It also didn't hurt that he was one of the hottest guys I'd ever laid eyes on.

I cleared my throat. I'd told Velma about the existence of Ram, but nothing else. I wasn't sure I was ready to. Plus, I didn't even know what I would say. I'd only spent a few hours with Ram so far . . . but already, a tiny spark lit up inside me every time I thought about him. Right now, in a way, he felt sacred, too, just like my writing.

Velma exhaled and dropped her binoculars. "This is exhausting. I can't believe how out of practice we are."

I nodded, yawned. The ground was hard and I shifted my butt, wincing. When we were kids, our stakeouts would last

DAPHNE

hours. We'd pop Swedish Fish and Skittles and M&M's to keep us going back then. I glanced longingly at The Mocha. Ram loved coffee, too, and I felt a lone butterfly begin to flap its wings inside my stomach. "What if we just grab a quick cup . . ."

Velma held up a hand. "Shh!"

I followed her gaze and froze. Down the block Shaggy had appeared, Scooby-Doo trotting next to him, as usual. Shaggy was in his trademark baggy pants and loose tee, his hair mussy and messy, looking like he'd slept funny. He had Scooby's leash in one hand and a muffin the size of my head in the other.

I scooted closer to Velma. We were pretty well-hidden to most passersby—not a lot of people were entering the movie theater at this time of day—but still, if Shaggy saw us (or, more likely, if Scooby caught a whiff of our scent) we'd have a tough time coming up with a plausible cover story.

We remained still as Shaggy and Scooby sauntered a few more feet before abruptly turning into a tiny store-front. I gaped and met Velma's eyes. She shrugged in response.

Antiques by Dee was a cramped, dusty antique shop that my mom had loved browsing in back when she lived here full-time; I hadn't been inside it since she moved to San Francisco years ago. If memory served, it had mostly held stuff from bygone eras: rickety lamps with dangerous-looking wiring, musty-smelling clothes, vintage dolls that looked like they would come alive at night. I shuddered. What on earth could Shaggy want in there?

Velma voiced what I was thinking. "Does Shaggy have an antiques habit we don't know about?"

I tried to imagine Shaggy collecting antiques. (It wasn't hard to do; his father's study was filled with old stuff, from Rogers family memorabilia to priceless artifacts like the famous Crystal Cove Crystal. Maybe antiquing as a hobby was genetic?) At the same time, a twentysomething couple rushed by, hand in hand, each of their faces trained on their phones. "Maybe Scooby has a thing for old fur coats?"

Velma tsked. I held up a hand; the last thing I needed was a lecture about animal cruelty. Suddenly, the door to the antique shop opened; a large brown nose poked out.

"Quiet," Velma mouthed.

"I know," I mouthed back.

Scooby and Shaggy stepped outside. Shaggy looked both ways, almost like he was deciding where to head next; then he made a left, Scooby trotting beside him, as they headed back the way they had come. Velma's fingers tightened around the binoculars.

Thwack! The door to the movie theater opened behind us; an employee—I guessed, judging by his black polo shirt

DAPHNE

with the movie theater logo on it—rushed out, bursting into a jog as he made a left. I jumped in surprise, hitting my elbow on the bench in front of us. I groaned, which made Velma hush me.

"Relax, he's too far away to hear us," I said hotly, rubbing my throbbing elbow.

She sighed. "I guess you're right. But look!"

Shaggy had paused in front of the gourmet grocery store.

"I guess everyone needs some fancy cheese once in a while?" Velma's voice was thick with doubt. We watched as the automatic doors swallowed him.

I suddenly remembered the turkey-and-cheese sandwich I'd eaten in the *Howler* break room the day before, and how, while I was eating, Ram had stopped in to get something from the office fridge. He'd nodded at my sandwich and said, his eyes twinkling, "Nice lunch, Blake."

"What's so funny?" Velma interrupted my memory.

"Oh, just something Ram . . ." My voice trailed off once I realized what I was about to reveal. Too late. Velma's eyes had lit up and she wiggled her eyebrows.

"Rammmmm?" She lingered on his name, mocking me. I couldn't help it—I burst out laughing. It felt good. Since Marcy had moved away with her parents, I'd been hanging out with Velma a lot, but we didn't usually talk about this kind of stuff. I'd missed it.

15

THE DARK DECEPTION

"Yes. Ram. I guess I . . . well, he's really . . . I mean . . ."

Velma nodded, smirking. "I'm sure he is."

"It's not like that!" I swore. "He's really . . . smart."

"*Smart?* Uh-huh."

The blush came fast and furious this time. I was powerless to hold it back. "Yes, smart. He can't help it if he's also . . . attractive."

I could see Velma was dying to say something, but we both paused when yet another person rushed by us, practically jogging, in the direction of the beach.

"What is going on?" I wondered.

The *whoosh* of the gourmet grocery's automatic doors interrupted us. We shrank back into our hiding spots—my butt was totally numb by this point—and Shaggy and Scooby bounded out. The muffin in Shaggy's hand was gone, but in its place was a cookie nearly as big as Velma's glasses.

"I guess he really was just . . . hungry?" she commented.

I shrugged. So far this stakeout was kind of a bust, and I was getting antsy.

But then Shaggy crossed the street and, quick as a flash, practically dove inside the jewelry store.

Now, I knew that jewelry store. Burnett's was a Crystal Cove institution—it had been run by the same family for years. Upon the elder Mr. and Mrs. Burnett's recent deaths, their middle-aged daughter, Noelle, had moved back to

16

town to run the place. It was where my dad got my sweet sixteen present (a nameplate necklace that I hadn't taken off since); it was where I'd bought Velma her tenth birthday present (a set of tiny amber studs that she still wore to this day). All the girls I knew browsed Burnett's before every big dance or special event.

I chewed the inside of my cheek. Shaggy didn't wear any jewelry, and he didn't have any piercings. (At least, none in plain sight.)

"Now we're getting somewhere," Velma muttered, her eyes glued to Burnett's.

"Are we, though?" I countered. "He could be in there for any number of reasons. The holidays are almost here, for example."

"Or maybe he has a secret girlfriend, like we thought!"

"I'm pretty sure that new freshman is Noelle's daughter," I added, chewing it over. "Maybe he likes her?"

"Oh, yeah, what's her name? Taylor? Tabitha?"

"Taylor," I confirmed. I'd noticed the new girl thanks, in part, to her tininess—she was short and thin and looked more like a sixth-grader than a freshman. At lunch, she seemed to spend her time skulking about the cafeteria, dubiously eyeing anyone who looked like they were having even a modicum of fun.

Noelle Burnett seemed fine, but her daughter sure felt like a downer, if you asked me.

THE DARK DECEPTION

Velma got a faraway look in her eyes. "Maybe . . ."

I could tell she was about to go off on some wild, and most likely wholly unfounded, tangent. I decided to get her back on track.

"Maybe Shaggy's buying Scooby an anklet!"

"Daphne." Velma gave me a look. "Why do I get the feeling you're not taking this seriously anymore?"

I sighed. Velma was right. Part of me was lost in a daydream involving me and Ram and some kind of disaster that led to us being the only two people stuck inside the *Howler* offices. I forced my thoughts back to what Marcy had written before she'd left town: *Shaggy needs your help.* I may not have fully understood the relationship Marcy and Shaggy had forged, but I knew enough about both of them to believe she wouldn't lie about that.

I was still processing the whole Shaggy/Marcy situation, to be honest. It had all started a few weeks ago when Marcy—my only best friend at the time, but now classified as my *other* best friend—had started acting super shady. Like, disappearing-for-entire-nights shady. Like, ignoring-my-texts-and-standing-me-up shady. Like, eventually-going-missing-altogether shady. I'd been desperate to find her—and luckily so was Velma, especially when other girls began disappearing. Together, we put our long-buried investigative skills to the test, eventually unearthing the real truth behind the disappearances.

DAPHNE

Throughout the whole ordeal, we discovered that Shaggy and Marcy had had some kind of relationship. Whether it was romantic or not, we couldn't be sure—neither was willing to explain—but it was, for sure, important to both of them. Fragile, even. And they were protective of it.

And that was why we were here, trying to track down Shaggy's movements on this glorious Saturday morning. Shaggy needed our help, and Marcy had asked us to help him.

We just needed to figure out why and how.

"Should we go inside? Corner him?" Velma pushed her glasses up. Again.

"First can we get you some contacts?"

"Daphne!"

"I'm being serious!" I gestured at her binoculars. "You'd have both hands free. And you'd be able to see better through those things."

She paused. "Well, my eye doctor did give me my contacts measurements at my last exam, so . . . I'll consider it. Now can we please move on?"

"Let's." I stood up. My knees creaked. "Oof. I need a yoga class, stat."

"Should we really go inside?" Velma straightened up, too. "That's not quite how I envisioned this stakeout ending . . ."

19

"You got any better ideas, Dinkley?"

We gathered our stuff, ignoring the questioning glances from a family that had emerged from the diner next door and noticed us creeping out from behind our hiding spot, and crossed the street.

Downtown Crystal Cove had grown quieter over the past few minutes; there were fewer people strolling the streets. Even The Mocha looked like it had cleared out. As we approached Burnett's, I cast a lingering glance in the shop window, where a collection of shiny bangles was calling my name. An unexpected thought rose up: Maybe one day, Ram would buy *me* a piece of jewelry from here . . .

Burnett's door jingled as Velma pulled it open. I followed her inside, blinking furiously as my eyes adjusted to the dim light.

"Welcome!" Noelle Burnett trilled from behind the register. A slight woman, probably in her forties, Noelle reminded me of every art teacher I'd ever had, with her loose, drapey clothing, layered necklaces, and cropped, tousled hair. Even though she'd left Crystal Cove before I was born, I vaguely knew her from her visits and from the family photos her parents had proudly hung throughout the store. She was practically the same size as her daughter—tiny and almost frail-looking, like a strong wind could knock her over. They had matching dark brown eyes, and Taylor even kind of dressed like her mom—which, I realized, was probably one

DAPHNE

of the reasons no one had really made friends with her yet. (In our high school, clothes mattered. A *lot*.) "What can I help you girls with today?"

"Um." Velma hesitated while I surveyed the store. Burnett's wasn't big, but with large jewelry displays towering in the middle of the floor, it was hard to get a full view of the place. Still, one thing was clear: Other than us, it was empty. Where had Shaggy and Scooby gone?

"Hi," I said warmly, sticking out my hand. "I remember you from your visits. I'm Daphne, and that's Velma. Your daughter is Taylor, right?"

Noelle's eyes lit up. "You know my Taylor?"

"Well, I've seen her around," I corrected, wincing as Noelle's face fell. Thinking fast, I pointed at the window display. "Hey, can you tell me more about those bracelets?"

Noelle smiled. "I knew all the cool young kids would love them! Taylor told me they would! Here, let me show you."

I tried not to roll my eyes—any time an adult called me a "cool young kid" I died a little inside—as Noelle fluttered over to me from behind the register. As she unlocked the case, Velma gave me an unidentifiable look, her eyes big and urging. I held up a finger to her. I had this under control. Jewelry was definitely my domain.

"Quiet morning?" I hoped my voice was casual.

21

Noelle finally opened the display case and pulled out the bracelets, leading me over to the register counter and meticulously laying out each one. "Oh, you know these gorgeous mornings. No one wants to be inside shopping!"

I noticed Velma step away and begin peering around the store. As Noelle insisted I try on the biggest, shiniest bracelet, Velma pretended to tie the laces on her boots, eyeing the space under the various tables sprawled across the room.

"Gorgeous," I said, admiring my wrist as the light glinted off the bangle. It really was a nice piece, and it would go perfectly with my new cashmere sweater. In fact, it would also be a great birthday gift for my mom. I felt like I really owed her something special this year, now that we were actually communicating in more than just angry, one-syllable fights.

"I can give you a discount," Noelle said eagerly.

But when Velma cleared her throat pointedly, I hurriedly put it back onto the counter and changed the subject. "Hey, so, I thought I saw Shaggy Rogers come in here a minute ago?"

Noelle blinked, her eyes bright and innocent. "Hmm, no, I don't think so."

I faltered. "Oh. I could have sworn . . ."

"So what do you think of these?" Noelle's expression changed as she gestured to the bracelets. "They look perfect on you."

I could feel Velma behind me. I knew her well enough to know that she'd finished scouring the store, and that, more importantly, she wasn't going to let Noelle change the subject so easily.

"They're really lovely," I said, pasting a sweet smile on my face. "But I, uh, forgot my wallet today."

"Me too," Velma interjected. "Actually, that's why we were looking for Shaggy. He, um, has my wallet."

Noelle frowned. "I thought you said you forgot it?"

"I did," Velma said quickly. She pushed her glasses up her nose and added, "At Shaggy's house. That's why he has it. And that's why I need him. *We* need him."

Noelle swiftly gathered up the bracelets. I noticed she was exerting an awful lot of concentration on spacing them out evenly. We were losing her. And Velma, I could sense, was losing patience.

"Noelle," I said quickly, placing a hand on the bracelet I'd tried on. "We saw Shaggy and Scooby-Doo come in here just a few minutes before we did. Can you at least tell us which direction they went? Because we didn't see them leave, and . . . well, we just need to talk to him. Please?"

She finally lifted her head and met my eyes. Her gaze was unwavering. "Shall I wrap this up for you? You can come back for it when you find your wallets."

I could feel Velma's scowl without even looking at her.

But I just smiled sweetly. Noelle was playing at something, and even though I didn't know what, I still knew how to play. You don't become the most popular girl in school without getting your hands a little dirty.

"Maybe some other time," I said warmly, pulling back my hand. "Maybe I'll ask around and see if the other kids at school like them as much as I do."

Noelle stiffened. But before she could reply, almost simultaneously, text alerts rang out from my and Velma's phones.

Velma was the first one to check. Her cheeks reddened as she did. She grabbed my elbow and I winced (it was the same elbow I'd whacked against the bench outside). "Follow me," she whispered, her voice low and urgent.

"Bye, Noelle," I called, pretending she hadn't just lied to our faces. She didn't meet my eyes as she waved us out.

In the sunlight, I squinted and waited until the door to the shop was firmly closed behind us. "Well, that was bizarre."

"We have bigger things to worry about," Velma hissed. She held up her phone. I peered at it. Then, gasping, I checked mine. While Velma's text was from her mom, and mine was from our classmate Sammie Daniels, they had the same overall message: **Get to the beach NOW. Something is happening!**

I heard feet pounding all around us. The Mocha's doors

were flung open; so were the gourmet grocery store's, and the diner's. People were flooding out into the streets, heading toward the beach. Some of them were running. All of them appeared frantic.

I felt a funny buzzing in my stomach; I reached out to grab Velma's arm. "Are you as scared as I am right now?"

"Hey!" Velma called to the next group of people that had piled out of the diner. It was Nisha Shah, Shawna Foster, Haley Moriguchi, and Trey Moloney; certainly people I'd think nothing of talking to. But I knew then that Velma was as worried as I was. Because Velma definitely wouldn't talk to them if she could help it, not unless she absolutely had to. "What's going on?"

"Didn't you hear?" Trey responded. He was halfway down the street already, and his voice rang out over the crowd. "It's the beach!"

"What about it?!" I called back. My heart was pounding now, adrenaline coursing through my veins.

Haley yelled something in response, but it was hard to hear her over all the noise. I felt a pang of anxiety. "Velma, did you hear what Haley said?"

Velma nodded and pushed her glasses up her nose. "Treasure," she said. "She said treasure has washed up on the beach."

VELMA

IN SEVENTH GRADE, HALEY Moriguchi plastered chewed-up gum all around the lock of my gym locker. Team sports were not my thing, even back then, and I returned to the locker room sweaty and grumpy and cursing our state's PE requirements, only to discover Haley's dirty trick.

She and her friends openly laughed while I tugged at the locker, tossing off witty remarks like "Looks like Detective Dinkley has a new case to solve—but nothing to wear while she solves it!" It took the cleaning staff two full periods to pry off that melted, sticky gum so I could change back into my regular clothes. By then, everyone in school had seen my legs in those horrible red shorts. And when I tried to report Haley to the principal, she denied it, even bursting into tears and pretending to be horrified by the very thought that someone like Velma Dinkley could think she, Haley Moriguchi, would ever do something so terrible.

It had been a bad year. Especially when I noticed Daphne laughing right along with Haley every time she saw me in the halls over the next few weeks.

Since then, Haley hadn't matured much. Even Daphne, who hung out with her a lot—especially during that looooong break in our friendship—could admit Haley wasn't the nicest of girls. "She has her good qualities," Daphne said, cocking her head, when I once asked about her. "I'm just not entirely sure she wants the world to see them."

So I'm not sure why Daphne was so surprised when I didn't believe Haley Moriguchi's claims of treasure. She wasn't exactly the most trustworthy of people.

Also, treasure doesn't just wash up on beaches, unless you're living in a fairy tale. And Crystal Cove was no fairy-tale setting. It was more like the backdrop of a horror movie.

Haley ran off with Nisha, Shawna, and Trey while Daphne and I tried to process what she could have meant. Or at least, I did. Because Daphne immediately made it clear that she was ready to grab a bucket and scoop up some of that so-called treasure.

"Let's go!" She pulled my elbow and began dragging me toward the direction of the beach.

"No way," I said. My voice was as firm as my legs, which were rooted to the ground.

Daphne pulled my arm. "Velma! I'm freaking out here!" Her voice was shrill as it echoed over the now-empty street.

"Come on," I protested. "Do you honestly believe that crap Haley is peddling?" I held still as Daphne readjusted her stance, trying to pull me down the street before finally relenting.

"We have to follow them!" she insisted.

My eyes glinted. "Since when are you a follower?"

I had her there. The Daphne Blake I knew—the *world* knew—was always leading the crowd. When we ran Mystery Inc., it was Daphne who convinced Shaggy and Fred to join us; it was Daphne who set the trends at school, who made the social plans, who decided which parties to hit up and which to avoid.

"But, V, clearly something is going on down at the beach. As a reporter for the *Howler*, it's my duty to go check it out. With or without you!" Daphne crossed her arms and glared at me.

"An *intern* reporter," I reminded her. But she had a point. Downtown Crystal Cove was empty now, as even the remaining stragglers streamed down the street. All the shops had locked up and flipped their signs to CLOSED (or, in the case of The Mocha, BE BACK SOON! DON'T MISS US

TOO MOCHA!). The normally bustling street suddenly looked like—well, I hated to say it, but like a ghost town. Like every resident had just decided to leave all at the same time, without even packing their bags.

Like everyone had just . . . vanished.

I raced to put the idea out of my head, but the Vanishing was never too far away from anyone's thoughts around here. How could it be, when it had never been solved? But that wasn't what was happening here, I reminded myself.

"What about Shaggy?" I countered. I gestured to the jewelry store behind us. "We saw him go in there. You know we did! And then Noelle flat-out lied to us. We have to get to the bottom of this!"

"Shaggy's probably down at the beach along with the rest of the world," Daphne offered. She glanced at her watch. "Listen, we will get to the bottom of the Shaggy mystery. But I'm going to the beach to see what's up, whether you come with me or not. So it's your call."

I stared at her. To her credit, she held firm, staring right back with that obstinate look on her face—the same one I'd watched her give to her parents whenever they forced her to stop whatever game we were playing (or, more likely, whatever mystery we were trying to solve at the time) when we were kids. Daphne Blake did what Daphne Blake wanted to do. She just had this miraculous way of making you think it was what *you* wanted to do, too.

"Fine," I caved. She squealed, and this time when she grabbed my elbow and pulled me along, I went with her.

We ran. I felt a little ridiculous running through town in combat boots; my head was starting to sweat underneath my beanie, and my face was so slippery that, halfway to the beach, I had to physically hold my glasses in place to keep them from flying off.

"Keep an eye out for Shaggy!" I reminded Daphne as we ran. She stopped short, and I crashed into her. "Oof! Daph!"

"Sorry," she panted. "But look. Whoa."

I pulled off my sweaty beanie and pushed up my glasses. *Whoa* was right.

Crystal Cove's beach was a glorious, mile-long stretch of white sand, capped on the northern side by a series of sea caves, and on the southern side by a jetty that jutted out into the waves. Summer was over but, this being California, it wouldn't be unusual for a few people to still be on the beach this time of year. Shaggy himself surfed year-round on this beach, and I scanned the water for him and his trademark orange wetsuit before realizing it was futile.

What looked like hundreds of people were packed onto the northern end of the beach, shielding their eyes from the sun and fighting their way to the water's edge. While some people hung back, Daphne and I dodged our way through bodies—even ducking under a few people who refused to give way for us—and, finally, reached the shoreline.

I pushed my glasses up my nose and blinked. Then, because there was obviously something wrong with them, I pulled them off, wiped the lenses against the hem of my hoodie, and pushed them back onto my face.

Nope. My glasses *had* to be broken. Because what I was seeing couldn't possibly be right.

"Oh. My. Sparkles," Daphne breathed.

"So it's not just me, then?" I barked out a bubble of nervous laughter.

"Haley was right!" Daphne pointed at the sea, which was about to deliver its next wave to the shore. And inside that wave was . . . treasure.

As the wave crashed gently onshore and then rolled its way up to our feet, swirling around my combat boots before receding, I stared. The sea was shining in a way that far surpassed the typical way it glinted from the sun's rays. I reached down, my fingertips brushing against the wet sand, and scooped up what the sea had deposited: a jewel.

More specifically, a ruby. A bloodred, craggy, sharp ruby nearly the size of a quarter; I identified the stone easily because it matched the stones in the vintage Mexican eagle ring my mother always wore, which had been her mother's and her grandmother's before that. It gleamed in the sunlight. Around us, floating in the waves, were

THE DARK DECEPTION

hundreds more: rubies, sapphires, emeralds, amethysts; all the colors of the rainbow in a place that should only be blue.

It felt like an offering. A gift. And wow, were the people of Crystal Cove happy to receive it. People were dashing into the sea, grabbing whatever jewels they could reach. I watched some of them carefully remove their shoes and roll up their pants; others just splashed right in, picking up jewels by the handful before emerging, dripping but triumphant, their pockets and palms overflowing. There was a jubilant feel to the air, as if the people of Crystal Cove had finally been handed some luck in the form of free jewels. As if they were saying, *Don't we deserve it, after all we've been through?*

My entire life, I'd heard about the cursed land from which the town of Crystal Cove blossomed. When an entire town vanishes, only to be burned to the ground a century later, let's just say *concerns* start to surface. And those worries linger, morphing into stories that are passed down through families until no one can tell what's true or not. Yes, Crystal Cove liked its legends, its ghosts—they were something to hang on to when we still didn't have any answers. And I couldn't deny this place had seen its fair share of ghosts. They just hadn't been the kind people tend to think of: instead of spirits, instead of withered old women in tattered, flowing cloaks and grizzled old men

32

VELMA

with their heads cut off, begging for revenge, it was more . . . a sense of foreboding. Of inevitable doom.

I'd learned a lot of lessons in my sixteen years. First and foremost: It wasn't my job to stop the people of Crystal Cove from thinking this town was haunted—not that I could (I should know; I tried for years). But I tried to help make sense of things whenever I could. And right now, that meant figuring out what was happening with these jewels.

"This is unreal!" Daphne trilled, scooping up the emeralds and sapphires that had floated over her feet. She'd ditched her boots and was ankle deep in the water now, an unnerving look of delight flooding her face.

My mind raced. It *was* unreal—in the literal sense. Reluctantly, I grabbed a couple more jewels and studied them in the sunlight. I didn't know much about gemstones (or any jewelry, for that matter), but these looked real enough.

"I'm only doing this for the investigation!" I called.

Daphne froze mid-pluck and then quickly recovered. "Me too, of course!"

"Attention! Attention!"

Shouts rang out over the crowd. It was hard to hear over the ocean and the roar of jewel-induced delight; it was hard to pinpoint where the calls for silence were coming from, especially as the beach grew more and more crowded.

THE DARK DECEPTION

I peered through bodies—my neighbors, my teachers, the kids at school—until I noticed the profile of Lieutenant Rogers, Shaggy's mother, with both hands waving, cutting through the sharp blue sky.

Shaggy! I remembered then that I'd meant to scan the crowd to see if he was here. While Lieutenant Rogers called for attention again, I looked, but I was too short to really see. I glanced enviously at Daphne. She had several inches on me, but she was busy comparing her jewels with Sammie Daniels's, who had waded over to us.

"Everyone, please stop!" Lieutenant Rogers yelled. She was standing on top of a large rock, probably to give herself some height, with a few of her officers surrounding her. The wind carried her voice to the outer edges of the crowd, and finally, most of us paused, straightened up, and directed our attention toward her. One of her officers handed her a megaphone, and she held it to her mouth before adding, "Thank you. Please, let's all take a minute and figure out what's going on here."

"We already know what's going on! Treasure!" someone shouted, and a roar rose up from a small circle of people still splashing in the waves.

Lieutenant Rogers held up a hand. "I understand you're all excited, and rightfully so—this is surely an unexpected morning! But we'd appreciate your cooperation in gathering up as many of these jewels as we can. It's imperative

VELMA

that we do our due diligence in understanding where these jewels came from so that we can, hopefully, get them back to their rightful owner."

I nodded in agreement even as several people around me grumbled. I felt a pang of sympathy for Shaggy's mother just then. It was not going to be easy to get some of this crowd to hand over the jewels they'd pocketed.

"Lieutenant! Care to go on the record with a statement?"

I stifled a groan as Milford Jones appeared, his swoop of blond hair and wide, open face nearly identical to that of his nephew, Fred Jones. He strode up to Shaggy's mom. Lanky and long, Milford was taller than Lieutenant Rogers, even as she remained on the highest rock on the shore.

"No statement at this time," she clipped. My heart pumped a little bit harder, and I grabbed Daphne's hand and began pulling her closer to the front of the crowd. I didn't want to miss a word.

Milford thrust a recorder in front of Lieutenant Rogers's face. "Nothing like this has ever happened here before, and the people deserve information."

Next to me, Daphne gasped. When I glanced at her, she looked like she'd seen a ghost: pale everywhere except for her cheeks, which were suddenly flushed, and her eyes, which were wide and shining. "That's Ram," she whispered.

THE DARK DECEPTION

I followed the direction of her stare. I hadn't noticed him at first, but once I did, I was shocked at my lack of observational skills. Ram was standing close to Milford, holding the same kind of recorder in his hands. He was definitely cute, and definitely way more sophisticated than the guys in school.

"Good taste, Daph," I muttered, and then yelped when she punched my shoulder in response.

"Don't embarrass me," she hissed.

"I appreciate your excitement, Mr. Jones," Lieutenant Rogers said in a voice indicating she did not, in fact, appreciate Milford's excitement.

Unsurprisingly, Milford didn't let up. He thrust his recorder even closer to Shaggy's mom. "Any thoughts on where these jewels came from?"

The neutral expression on Lieutenant Rogers's face flickered. She forced a small—but definitely fake—smile. I'd never felt closer to Shaggy's mother; I, too, had noticed how my general distaste for Milford Jones was always entirely too visible on my own face. I didn't know how Daphne was managing to work for him. He oozed a certain smarmy used car salesman vibe that always set me on edge.

"Maybe a cruise ship passing by, or some kind of freight delivering goods to the next port up the coast," she suggested.

Everyone turned to scan the horizon line. I don't know

what they were expecting to see—ships? A giant banner that read GIVE ME BACK THOSE JEWELS? But the horizon was clear, except for a few hazy clouds that drifted lazily through the sky.

"What if the people don't want to surrender the items they've collected?" Milford pressed. Shouts began to rise from the back of the crowd.

"Yeah!"

"Right on!"

"They're mine!"

People jostled; waves continued to roll up the beach, leaving more and more jewels in their wake. Within seconds, the relatively calm crowd had grown riled and restless. Lieutenant Rogers called for quiet again, but small factions of the crowd had begun to yell back at her, protesting and shouting out their ideas for what to do with all these jewels.

"Please! We need everyone to remain calm!" Lieutenant Rogers's voice echoed over the beach, but it was increasingly drowned out by shouts from the crowd.

"These washed up on *our* beach!" someone yelled, and a round of applause broke out at her words.

"I'm keeping mine," someone else hollered, shrugging as if the situation were out of his hands. "I found them fair and square."

"Me too!"

"Us too!"

"Yep, these are ours!"

"Well, this isn't great," Daphne murmured.

The unfortunate thing about anger is that it's usually contagious. When someone in front of me pointed a furious finger at Shaggy's mother and nearly elbowed me in the face, I felt it swirl around my insides, too. "Relax!" I snapped.

"Okay . . ." Daphne said, leading me toward the outskirts of the crowd and away from the center of the action. "Let's not get into a fight here on the beach, all right?"

"Look at these people," I fumed. The crowd was at least two hundred strong by now, and most of them appeared ready to stand their ground. Lieutenant Rogers and her other officers were now pleading with people to settle down, to turn over their jewels. "What is this, grade school? You don't get to play finders keepers with stuff this valuable!"

"Look!" Daphne said.

I forced myself to look away from the protestors to discover that Shaggy had taken over his mom's perch on the jetty. He was waving his arms around, practically jumping up and down to get the crowd's attention. It was a moment I'd never forget—a rare time Shaggy's hands were empty, absent of any food.

"Like, hey! Listen up!" Shaggy cupped his hands around

his mouth to yell, and then whistled. The long, piercing sound echoed through the beach and brought everyone—well, nearly everyone, I noticed, watching as Milford Jones continued hounding Lieutenant Rogers—to a standstill.

"Everyone. Like, please. Can we just take a minute?" Shaggy's voice was loud, thanks to the megaphone one of his mom's officers had handed over to him, but I could hear a tremble underneath. This was big for Shaggy; he didn't like being the center of attention.

The rest of Crystal Cove must have realized how serious he was at the same time, because most people paused to listen. Shaggy rubbed his head, tugged at his green T-shirt.

"What?" someone from the crowd asked.

"Like . . . yikes!" Shaggy started. He opened his arms as if he were embracing us all. "Is this who we are? A town that steals things that don't belong to us?"

A voice from deep within the center of the group yelled, "What if they *do* belong to us?"

Shaggy shrugged. "Like, okay. But all we know is they washed up ashore. That doesn't make them ours."

Behind me, a throat cleared. I turned and found myself face-to-face with Mr. Rogers, Shaggy's father. And he was scowling at his son.

I whipped my head back around and whispered to Daphne, "Mr. Rogers, behind us, seven o'clock. And he does not look happy."

Daphne surreptitiously swiveled her head, her shiny red hair providing cover for her eyes, which scanned Mr. Rogers. He was a stern-looking man; though I'd known him most of my life, I couldn't remember a single time I'd seen him smile, a single moment when he'd appeared relaxed, at ease.

This morning was no different. His craggy face, all sharp angles and flat planes, was trained on his son, his eyes narrowed. A set of scowl lines, identical parentheses above his nose, deepened. Whatever he was hearing, it almost looked like it was making him ill. I knew Shaggy and Mr. Rogers had a bit of a rough relationship, but it was only then, in the bright glare of the morning sunshine, that I realized just how rough. It was plain for the world to see.

A pang of pity for Shaggy thrummed at my stomach. Within seconds it had morphed into concern. What was Mr. Rogers even doing here? The guy was always so busy, so mired in his many business meetings, so *important*, that he never made time for Shaggy. He'd skipped every back-to-school night, every birthday party, every end-of-year awards ceremony that Shaggy had been invited to.

So, I wondered, openly staring at Mr. Rogers, why now? What was he doing here on the beach?

It could only mean this was way more serious than I'd initially thought. Right?

I chewed my lip as I tore my eyes away from Mr. Rogers.

Now Shaggy and Milford Jones were going at it, with Milford lobbing questions at Shaggy until Lieutenant Rogers stepped forward to bear the brunt of Milford's storm. The whole thing felt like a volleyball match. (See? This is why I hate team sports.)

Milford continued. "What if I can prove they are the rightful property of the residents of Crystal Cove?" His recorder veered dangerously close, in my opinion, to the lieutenant's face. I scoffed, but the crowd was hanging on to his every word. I'll give him one thing: Milford knew how to play to an audience. I guess that was why the *Howler* had such a loyal readership, even though some of us— ahem, me—didn't view it as much more than a gossip rag. And most of it incorrect gossip, at that.

Lieutenant Rogers squinted and pushed Milford's recorder out of her face. Smooth, Lieutenant. "How could you possibly prove that, Milford?"

"Because," he responded, his voice pleasant and easy, belying his words, "it's pretty clear to anyone who knows our history. Many families have passed down stories about the valuable items that went missing when the original set-tlers vanished. Our ancestors came here looking for their missing relatives, and we have long kept lists of the missing items . . . including, notably, jewelry."

Lieutenant Rogers gritted her teeth. "What specifically are you trying to say, Mr. Jones?"

"It's obvious, Lieutenant." A thin smile curled up Milford's face. "What if," he asked, visibly relishing the crowd's anxiety, "what if these jewels are from the vanished settlers of Crystal Cove?"

Almost in unison, the crowd gasped.

I couldn't stop the shiver that raced up my spine. Even here, in the broad daylight, surrounded by people, I could feel the weight of his words, the weight of the memory of the departed. It was impossible not to. It was, I realized with a sickening pang, what would always be the invisible guest in every conversation held here; the uninvited visitor lurking around every corner. Crystal Cove's most famous fact: We were a town whose people had vanished. A place where the questions outweighed the answers; where, no matter what we'd go on to achieve, to build, to create, we would always have to answer for the asterisk that dotted our name in every mention. Because no matter what we did in the future, Crystal Cove still hadn't found answers for our past.

Which meant it was all too easy for people like Milford Jones to leverage the Vanished to get what they wanted.

"He's right," a person next to me whispered.

"Don't be ridiculous," I muttered.

But it was too late. A murmur was growing, rising from a whisper to a steady drumbeat that soon overtook the noises from the waves, from the traffic over the south end of the beach on the only highway out of town. I heard a distant car honk. I wished, desperately, to be in that car. Driving away from Crystal Cove, away from the ghosts we couldn't seem to shake.

And then Mr. Rogers, iridescent in his anger, stepped forward and ripped the recorder out of Milford's hand. Shaggy shrank back, step by step, until he disappeared into the crowd.

"I'm on it," Daphne said. "I'll go find him!" She flashed a smile at me and disappeared into the crowd. It was a good call on her part, I thought as I caught glimpses of her red hair racing up the beach. Daphne could get anyone, even someone as closed off as Shaggy, to talk to her—a quality I definitely did not possess. It's what made her so good at this stuff.

"Jones," Mr. Rogers seethed. A gust of wind whipped through the cove, lifting his salt-and-pepper hair off his face.

Milford leaned in eagerly, always chasing the story. "Yes, Mr. Rogers?" His response was almost lyrical, musical, in its glee. The man loved nothing more than to rile people up. Passion fueled newspaper sales.

"It's that kind of absurd, preposterous claim that makes people look down on this town." Holding the recorder, Mr. Rogers's knuckles were white.

"Do you have any other theories, Samuel? Or did you

just want to state for the record that you disagreed with mine?" Milford gestured behind him. "Ram, you better be taking notes."

Mr. Rogers took another step closer to Milford. The two were nose to nose. The last thing this town needed was a head-on collision of testosterone, so without thinking it through, I ducked under shoulders and in between legs before popping up next to them.

"Gentlemen," I said. I pushed up my glasses—partly to stall for time and partly because the stupid things had slid down my nose. Again.

Neither Mr. Rogers nor Milford noticed me. I tried again. I was used to being invisible at school, among my peers, but I wouldn't stand for it here. Besides, I could deal with adults. I'd always found them easier to talk to, to manage.

It was teenagers my own age I had a problem with.

"Ahem." I cleared my throat. Mr. Rogers shot a disdainful glance my way. I'd take it, since it meant—hopefully—his rage was dissipating. I seized the moment. "This isn't really helping the lieutenant . . ."

"That's enough, Velma." Speaking of the lieutenant, she had sneaked up on me. She snapped her fingers, all business. "Let the adults handle this."

"Because you're all doing such a great job at it?" I muttered, stomping a few steps back. Heat pooled in my cheeks.

"Your theory is completely baseless," Mr. Rogers

reprimanded Milford. His tone triggered a memory, and I flashed back to one of those unending, too-hot days the summer we were ten. The heat wave had made it unbearable to be outdoors, even at Fred Jones's pool, so Daphne, Shaggy, Fred, and I had all escaped to the Rogers mansion, where the never-ending corridors were chilly from air-conditioning and all opened up to room after room. We'd been taking a break from a rousing game of Clue, making ice cream sundaes out of everything—anything!— we could find in the kitchen, when Mr. Rogers roared into the room and accused us of making too much noise. The look he was giving Milford Jones now was the same one he'd aimed at us that day.

I swore to myself right then and there that, no matter what Shaggy's secret turned out to be, I'd never go to his father for help. Never.

"Not just baseless. Dangerous. You thrive on feeding people false information just so you can sell more papers."

Milford's face changed, a fleeting expression of panic crossing it before it settled into its usual gloating look again. "Go on."

"Your . . . accusation is about as believable as . . . as . . ." Mr. Rogers looked wildly around, as though his metaphor were floating through the air and he needed to catch it. "As saying these jewels are the same ones stolen by the Lady Vampire of the Bay!"

Oh, great. Just fabulous. How did Shaggy's father always know exactly the wrong thing to say? Because if Milford was getting the crowd riled up by mentioning the Vanished, Mr. Rogers was about to get them downright *terrified* by mentioning the Lady Vampire of the Bay.

As his words rippled through the crowd, I got my defense ready. Yes, Crystal Cove had lots of legends and myths—like most towns, I would argue. And while the Vanishing was our most famous, there were many others, ranging from absolutely impossible to maybe, kind of, sort of feasible. And the myth of the Lady Vampire of the Bay was definitely the former.

I tried to remember what I knew for sure about her: One fall day, many decades ago, some kids playing at the beach swore they saw a ghost wandering through the caves, up and down the shoreline. She had long red hair and a purple cape, and they claimed she was floating, flying over the water with rage in her eyes. The kids ran away, screaming for help.

When the police investigated, though, they found no evidence anyone had been at the bay. But soon, others in town began to report strange occurrences—claims of appearances of a mysterious red-and-purple lady nearby, wandering through the village and walking on the waves. There was a rash of break-ins at around the same time, with jewelry stolen from some of the wealthiest women in town. Soon enough, people started theorizing that the Lady Vampire of the Bay was behind the thefts, and anything that went wrong in Crystal Cove was thought to be her work. Even now, every autumn, at least one kid would try to summon her with a midnight séance on Halloween night. Lieutenant Rogers was onto them, though, and she stationed an officer near the caves every Halloween.

In other words, the Lady Vampire of the Bay was ... nothing. Just a story some kids told that got out of hand.

Like things were about to get here.

DAPHNE

WHO KNEW SHAGGY WAS this fast? I made a mental note to tell him to try out for the track team once I finally found him. *If* I ever found him.

The truth is, I gave up looking pretty quickly. (Though I would never admit that to Velma.) Who can blame me? By the time I made it up the beach, my calves were burning from the effort and the soles of my feet were burning from the hot sand. The crowd was packed tight, and all that weaving and bobbing to find an open path meant that, once I reached the parking lot, not only was I exhausted—I thought longingly of The Mocha and its closed door—but Shaggy was also long gone. Completely out of sight. Almost like he . . . vanished.

Okay, maybe an unfortunate choice of words. Little did

DAPHNE

I know that the Vanished were all anyone was talking about back on the beach. Well, the Vanished and the Lady Vampire of the Bay, that ghost all the older kids at school used to try to scare us with when we were kids. One year, probably my peak year of fear, around age seven, the bigger kids at my bus stop even started making fun of me, saying I looked just like the Lady Vampire, thanks to my red hair.

Once I knew Shaggy was gone, I did a 180 and ran right back onto the beach. I've always had this thing about being in the middle of the action. It's always made me feel . . . I don't know. *Important* isn't the right word for it. More like *involved*. Like if I'm right there in the thick of things, then that means I can't be anywhere else. Like, just for instance, *alone*, lost in my head. Because I hate getting lost in my head.

Plus, well, Ram was there.

I pushed Ram out of my mind and trotted back to where I'd left Velma. Except she was gone! She'd left our spot, too. Luckily, I didn't have to look for her long. She'd made herself pretty obvious, standing up there on the jetty as Shaggy's parents faced off against Milford. Cool—my friend's dad and my boss were about to get into a fight, by the looks of things. And our stakeout was a bust, and Noelle had lied to my face, and I hadn't even had coffee yet. This weekend was turning out *spectacularly*.

I dodged to the front of the crowd again and waved my

arms up and down in an attempt to get Velma's attention. Eventually it worked, but not before I heard all about how the jewels littering the beach were from the Vanished, ancient artifacts bestowed to the people of Crystal Cove by a bunch of ghosts. Then I heard that no, actually, the jewels were from the Lady Vampire, who was haunting our little town again, desperate to find the jewels she'd heisted so long ago. One thing was clear: In this crowd, factions were forming quickly. Ugh, I had a lot to catch up on.

"Everyone, please! Keep calm!" Lieutenant Rogers shouted. She'd finally regained the crowd's attention. "The police department has set up collection areas all around the beach. Please deposit the jewels you've found on your way out. Of course, people are welcome to stay and continue collecting. As you can see, there are still a few more coming in with the tide."

While I waited for Velma, I scanned the sea. The sheen of jewels cresting with the waves had definitely thinned, and a couple dozen people still stood in knee-high water and scooped up whatever they could grab. Some of the crowd had started to dissipate, too, dropping their jewels off as they did, and grumbling the whole time.

"Blake!" Aparna Din collided into my shoulder, breathless. "Oh em gee, I'm so glad I ran into you. Isn't this scary?!"

I crinkled my nose. It was a picture-perfect fall day, and we were on a beach surrounded by people. "Scary?"

DAPHNE

"You know." Her voice dropped and she leaned in. I glimpsed genuine fear in her shining eyes. For a moment I began to grow scared myself; a flicker of panic threaded its way up my throat. Had something horrible happened to Aparna? "These jewels. At first I thought it was so cool! Like, what luck, right?"

She shook her head and then, to my utter shock, wiped the beginning of a tear from her eye. It was almost like we were having two separate conversations, that's how confused I was. The panic in my throat made way for something else: disdain.

"But now . . . all this talk about the Vanished. And ghosts. And . . . I mean . . . what if these jewels are cursed, Daph? Now they just feel like a bad omen."

She hugged me, squeezing my shoulders tight, and then added, "Whatever this is, we'll get through it. Together. Right?" And then she was off.

I stared after her for a moment, speechless, until I noticed the new girl, Taylor Burnett, was nearby, looking at me with an odd expression. I blinked, cleared my throat, and pulled myself together. I was used to people studying me, but the intensity of her gaze was a bit unsettling. "Can I help you?" I asked.

She twisted her mouth, looking like she was going to say something, but then turned and walked back into the crowd.

THE DARK DECEPTION

"What was that all about?" Velma asked. She'd unzipped her hoodie; it was the beachiest I'd ever seen her look. I glanced down and sighed to see her combat boots were still tightly laced. I guessed even Beachy Velma had her limits.

"The strangest thing," I told her, and relayed my conversation with Aparna and the odd moment with Taylor. "I know I was gone for a hot second, but do you think people are actually scared of these jewels?"

"Based on what I'm hearing? Yep." Velma ticked off her fingers. "First your boss brings up the Vanished—which, as you know, reminds this town that we live on top of a mystery that's never been solved. Then Shaggy's dad brings up the Lady Vampire of the Bay, and even though everyone here knows that's just a silly legend, it gets them thinking about ghosts, and hauntings, and spirits, and the unexplained."

"And we just went through a 'haunting,'" I added. "It almost doesn't matter that it turned out to be Aunt Emma and Dr. Hunter kidnapping people!" I sniffed. I didn't like to think about how Aunt Emma—my mom's best friend (or, rather, former best friend)—had betrayed us, had lied to us. She and Dr. Hunter were responsible for blackmailing and ultimately kidnapping my other best friend, Marcy, along with a few other kids from town. I didn't let a lot of people get close to me. Aunt Emma had been one of the few, and I had paid for that mistake.

"People just remember the fear," Velma confirmed. "And now . . . it looks like it's going to happen all over again."

We took a moment to study the scene at the beach. By now, more than half the people had deserted the area; the police officers were still stationed along the perimeter, carefully—or, I noted, in some places, care*less*ly—placing the washed-up jewels into buckets someone had dug out of the lifeguard headquarters. Those who remained were milling about the water's edge, kicking at the waves and digging toes through sand to make sure nothing had been overtaken by the tide. Taking the concept of "buried treasure" a little too literally, I guessed.

But most of all, what we noted about the crowd that remained was the whispers. People spoke to each other in hushed tones; they shot darting, nervous glances at their neighbors. Lieutenant Rogers was saying what looked like goodbye to Shaggy's dad—knowing him, he was probably off on yet another business trip—and the panic in my throat thrummed, salty and vivid, when the kid from the movie theater we'd seen earlier jostled his recovered jewels in his hands and muttered, "I can't believe anyone would think these are from a cruise ship."

His friend, who I recognized as one of the baristas from The Mocha, nodded. "Honestly, bro, I'm happy to give these back. I don't want haunted stuff in my house!"

THE DARK DECEPTION

I met Velma's eyes. She pushed up her glasses. In a rush of impatience, I pulled them off her nose.

Her face registered surprise, anger, and then, finally, acceptance. "Fine," she said, surrendering. "I'll get some contacts."

Then she took back the glasses, unfolded them, and placed them on her nose. "But until then, I definitely won't be able to see any ghosts without them."

* * *

The only bad part about my internship was the Sunday morning shift. Of course, seeing Ram pounding away at his keyboard when I arrived at the *Howler* offices made things slightly better. I ducked my head as I rounded the cubicles; I would die if anyone else noticed me looking at him.

It was both great and awful luck that Milford made the interns sit together in the same section. I placed my monogrammed leather tote on my chair, forcing myself to focus on my immediate line of vision, pretending that my body hadn't noticed and already registered the existence of Ram, the closeness of him. He was right there; I could reach out and—

"Blake!"

My head snapped; my heart leapt. "Yes?" I said too quickly. My mouth was a desert and I chugged my iced coffee but then, because I'm apparently an utter child, choked on it.

As I coughed and sputtered, Ram began pounding on

my back, like I was some kind of baby. My eyes watered. Part of me was ready to just give in and start fully crying, since who would know? I was botching this so hard already, why not go all in?

But Daphne Blake would never. I had a reputation to uphold, no matter how ill-conceived it was. Ram's back pounding (well, it was really just a tapping; despite his visible sleek strength, he wasn't a brute) had done the trick. I stopped coughing and forced back my tears. When I cleared my throat, I attempted a smile, but meeting Ram's eyes head-on without turning purple was still a feat I hadn't managed to accomplish.

It had been ten days since I'd first laid eyes on Ram, and I hadn't yet been able to figure out what specifically it was about him that made me feel like I was unmoored, like my feet weren't touching the ground. After my first day on the *Howler* staff, when we'd shaken hands and, palm burning, I'd had to excuse myself to the restroom— I'd needed to go somewhere private to process his face, his existence—I'd rushed home to do some research. Here's what I discovered:

- Ram was a freshman at the small but ritzy Hartwood College, which was located a few miles outside town; he'd grown up on the East Coast and returned there often to visit his family.

- He had two little sisters back home, still in elementary school . . . and, based on the photos I'd found, they had him utterly wrapped around their fingers.
- He was majoring in journalism and, in addition to his *Howler* internship, he worked at his college newspaper while also carrying a full course load.
- It appeared, based on the photos he shared on social media, that he didn't have a girlfriend. (Or a boyfriend, but I was really hoping he was more the girlfriend type. Because I was the boyfriend type, and I wanted desperately to tell him that. You know, without sounding creepy.)

This was just me doing my due diligence, I told myself that night. Now that I worked at the *Howler*, I needed to seek out the facts. It was my *job* to investigate my coworker. That was my story, at least, and I was sticking to it. All those walls I'd carefully erected around myself years ago, back when Velma and I had our big fight and my mom left me and my dad? They'd sunk deep into the ground, their foundations growing stronger and stronger. They felt impossible to tear down. The idea that I could let someone else venture inside them, even if just for a moment, made my heart race. The Daphne Blake everyone knew, the one I meticulously crafted, was confident and smooth and entirely self-sufficient. She needed no one but herself.

I just hadn't realized that one day she'd feel so entirely alone. Even with Velma back at my side, even with my relationship with my mom back on track, I felt like I lived on a boat alone in a sea where I could see people on the shore but couldn't quite figure out how to reach them. And lately, I'd really been wondering what it might be like to count on someone else. To let them in.

After I'd finished choking, I placed my bag on my desk and resisted the urge to crawl under my seat; instead, I sat down and crossed my legs.

"You good?" Ram asked. I nodded, still unable to look at him. Instead I focused really hard on powering up the rickety old computer the *Howler* had provided for me. It took at least five full minutes to begin functioning properly, which I was grateful for this morning, because I needed at least that much time to get over the spectacle I'd just made of myself.

But Ram had other ideas. He rolled his chair over to my desk. I caught a whiff of what was maybe cologne or, more likely, was just his own organic scent: soapy, piney, with a tinge of salt from the sea air. I breathed it in and then, conscious that I probably looked pathetic, I straightened my back and put on the Daphne mask I wore best: blank, unreadable, neutral but still pretty enough to trick everyone into thinking I was on their team. It was safe, that mask. I knew how to work it, and it had always served me well.

THE DARK DECEPTION

"What's up?" I said coolly. I wanted another sip of my coffee, but I wasn't eager to make a fool of myself again, so it sat, sweating, on my desk.

Ram tapped the little reporter's notebook he always carried around. (I'd purchased three of them after seeing his during my first day on the job. Not that I would ever admit that.) "New assignment from Milford. We're supposed to work on it together. And warning: He's on the warpath."

I raised my eyebrows. I'd had a hard time explaining to my mother that I'd be working at the *Howler*. Heck, I'd had a hard time justifying it to myself when I'd been selected. The *Howler* was mostly harmless gossip, sure, but it had a mean streak. Its specialty was in trying to take down the famous Elizabeth Blake. Every year, almost like clockwork, the *Howler* printed some kind of wild theory about my mother, about how her gaming empire was really a dastardly, devious plan to ruin Crystal Cove. Milford hated *The Curse of Crystal Cove* with every fiber of his being, and he made sure that came across in his editorials, and in the sometimes downright sleazy way he'd allow certain articles about my mom to be positioned. Why, I wasn't quite sure—if anything, my mother's game had helped cement Crystal Cove's legend, and Milford milked our spooky reputation for all it was worth. In fact, I'd wager that Milford Jones wouldn't even *have* a newspaper if not for my mother.

In other words, in my opinion, Milford owed his current career to her.

Maybe, I thought as Ram scratched at a spot on his upper arm that made me nearly reach out and caress it, that was why he hated her so much.

"Why?" I asked, keeping my voice casual. If Ram knew who my mother was, he didn't let on. Good. I didn't want him to know just yet; I liked conveying an air of mystery.

"Well, after yesterday's discovery at the beach, and then all the reports that came in overnight, he wants a roundup of quotes from residents, stat."

I frowned. "Wait, what reports that came in overnight?"

Ram's eyes, already big and brown, widened even more. "Blake. Haven't you heard?" He leaned over and clicked my mouse a few times.

I tore my eyes away from him and onto the computer screen. He'd pulled up the police blotter that had been published just this morning. My eyes skimmed over the list. With every bullet point, my jaw dropped a little farther.

At dusk, there was a sighting of a red-haired woman in a purple cloak near the entrance to the sea caves—and the witness was sure it was the Lady Vampire of the Bay. Around eleven p.m., there were three separate reports from families who lived on or near Beach Street, each claiming to see mysterious lights twinkling on the water.

An hour later, two families—one residing downtown and one uptown—each reported hearing loud popping noises. (It turned out the streetlights on their respective streets had blown out.) At three in the morning, a family called to report a break-in, but when police appeared, the house didn't show any signs of forced entry and no items were missing (though the owners did claim their jewelry boxes had been rifled through).

The blotter, normally a two-to-three-item list, continued with another half dozen similar reports: an elderly woman calling to report "shadows that didn't belong" in her hallway, some twentysomethings in the new high-rise condos downtown reporting a smoky haze ("reminiscent of ghosts," the report said) in their apartment building's garage; multiple calls about strange noises. And then, at dawn: A woman out for an early run called to report a "ghost ship" lurking on the sea near the caves. When police arrived, she was frantic, but the horizon was clear.

I exhaled a breath I hadn't realized I'd been holding. This was the biggest spike in crime Crystal Cove had ever seen. Or "crime," I should say, because I wasn't sure if "ghost ship sightings" counted as criminal. Regardless, it was clear ghosts were on everyone's mind. Crystal Cove was spooked.

"So I'm thinking you and I head over to that coffee shop, maybe to some of the restaurants, the parks," Ram continued. "I bet we'll find a lot of people willing to talk about ghosts."

I nodded. "Oh, we definitely won't have trouble finding people to talk about ghosts."

Ram raised his left eyebrow. I hesitated. My stomach felt like it was folding in on itself; like a sinkhole had formed. I was nervous, I realized. I wasn't sure how much Ram knew about this place, and I was going to have to tell him all of it: How, sometimes, it felt like more ghosts lived in Crystal Cove than people. How the stories about our history often felt more important, more *real*, than the actual goings-on of our lives. How Crystal Cove's legends were alive and well, even though the rest of the world had long since moved on.

"You know about this place, right?" I decided to start off slowly. Around us, all the rings and beeps and swooshes of office life provided a backdrop, a normal-enough sound-scape that helped me feel like what I was about to say wasn't so . . . weird.

"I mean, I know it's a tourist town that's undergoing rapid growth." He shrugged, his pen hovering over his notebook. "Why? You think there's an angle we should take in our story there?"

I held up a hand. "No. I mean, I don't know. Whatever you think. I just wanted to make sure you knew what you were getting into."

"Sure," Ram said agreeably. "It's a tale as old as time. A town changing, and some of its people reluctant to embrace the change."

It was true Crystal Cove was changing. Charming, rickety old row homes jutted up against glitzy new office buildings; families like the Rogerses, who had been here for generations, now mingled with new families who brought with them new ideas and expectations of what this place should be. The buyers of various plots of land throughout town had to follow the rules—to respect the town's character and use the land in some way that celebrated Crystal Cove—but those rules were easy to get around in court, and in practice. We had fancy coffee shops and co-working spaces now, but despite them, and despite the influx of people and commerce, there was a part of Crystal Cove that would always remain just as it began: the site of a mass mystery. Or, as some would say: a cursed land.

"It's more than that." I drummed my fingers against my desk, noticing Ram's were resting there, too. "It's like . . . well, there's a reason the thing at the beach yesterday got this town so . . . nervous."

Now both of Ram's eyebrows rose. "You can't mean that stupid thing Milford said, right? Or that other guy? The businessman?" Ram scoffed. "They were clearly joking."

I winced. "Um. Not really."

DAPHNE

Here's the thing: How do you explain to someone who didn't grow up in Crystal Cove what it's like here? About how Crystal Cove's cursed past made some people believe in a cursed future, too? As kids, Velma, Shaggy, Fred, and I would go on haunting expeditions in Shaggy's creepy house. Velma's family led tours about our history, about the Vanished. We Blakes had ghosts to thank for the roof over our heads and the beautiful clothes in our closets. Mystery was part of our land, and part of us.

I decided it would be easier—and likely more effective—to *show* Ram what I meant, rather than tell him. Let him hear firsthand what the people of Crystal Cove thought.

"How about this? We both hit the downtown areas together to get some quotes from people. Then we split up—I can go back to the beach, maybe? I bet there are people hanging out there, waiting for more jewels to wash up. And you can hit up Noelle Burnett. She owns the jewelry shop in town. I bet she'll give you a good quote."

It was strategic, my plan. I didn't think Noelle would give me anything after yesterday's little stunt in her store. Maybe Ram would be able to find out what she was hiding.

"Good plan, Blake." Ram nodded, jumping to his feet. He was dressed in what I'd come to think of as his typical weekend wear: a funny T-shirt and hipster jeans topped with a vintage plaid blazer. And, of course, his trademark orange sneakers. Somehow, it all worked. I glanced down at my own outfit—denim jacket over a plain tank top and a pencil skirt, plus the same boots I'd worn yesterday—and couldn't stop the flash of wonderment at how we would look together, like as partners. Or a couple.

"Right," I said, flustered at the thought. In my haste to act casual I nearly knocked over my coffee while reaching for my bag, but then Ram grabbed it, saving me from spilling it all over myself.

"I've never seen someone have so many run-ins with caffeine." Ram grinned at me.

I hated to admit it, but I positively soared our whole trip downtown, just from that single moment.

VELMA

"JINKIES!"

I tiptoed into my parents' bedroom, expertly avoiding the creaks in the floor so as not to scare my cat. Their bed was neatly made, and they were both out for the morning; this was a new habit they'd gotten into over the past few weeks, which I was grateful for. My dad has had depression for a couple of years now. Seeing him get out of the house more often was something I'd desperately hoped for, but hadn't believed would ever actually happen again.

"Gotcha!" I yelped, dropping to the floor and lifting up the bedspread. When Jinkies wasn't following me around, she was usually right here, under my parents' bed, pawing at the remains of a toy.

Huh. There was nothing there.

THE DARK DECEPTION

Frowning, I stood up, brushing off my jeans. Jinkies usually slept cuddled up next to me, but something had spooked her in the middle of the night, and she'd darted off. Normally, finding her would be a matter of minutes—with such a tiny apartment, there weren't many options for her to hide—but now, with towering piles of moving boxes scattered everywhere, there was somehow less space than usual, but many more places to disappear.

I moved through each room, calling Jinkies's name. And in each room, silence greeted me. Well, silence and mounds of cardboard. Even the echoes in here were different now. I couldn't wait to move out of this apartment—it had never felt like home, would always be the place things fell apart—but ugh, this transition period was the worst. My bedroom (which was really more of a closet) was the only place free from boxes and mess, and that's only because Mom and I had agreed that there simply wasn't enough room to store anything in there.

Finally, I made my way to the kitchen, taking a moment to enjoy the lingering smell of last night's enchiladas, and rattled the bag of kitty food, making as much noise as possible. Jinkies was a sucker for a snack.

"Come on, Jinkies!" I tried again. "Don't make me search through all these boxes!"

While I waited for Jinkies to slink back out of whatever hiding place she'd discovered, I checked my phone. I had a new text from Daphne: **Meet me downtown when you get up. I've got a scoop!**

I smiled. Ever since Daphne had started her internship, she'd incorporated phrases like "I've got a scoop!" and "Breaking news!" into her lexicon. It was charming on her, but if anyone else tried to do it, it would quickly become annoying.

"Jinks!" I tried again, rattling the bag even louder. I searched for the next twenty minutes, to no avail. And that's when I started to get nervous. Jinkies had never disappeared like this; sure, we liked to play hide-and-seek, but our game had never lasted this long before, and she nearly always came when I called. I double-checked that all the windows were properly closed—they were—and then I did the next best thing I could think of: I called my mom.

"Hola, mi amor," she said when she picked up. In the background, I could hear utensils clinking and music playing. Ah, the diner. I smiled at the sounds, even though my dad was basically a walking meme: "Visits New Jersey once, becomes expert on diners." It was nice to see him enjoying the things he loved again.

Ever since the deed confirming my family owned the large plot of land in the middle of Crystal Cove had been found—the deed that showed we did, in fact, own the house we used to live in back before we got kicked out and the lot was turned into the Haunted Village amusement park—he'd been happier; brighter. Like the dimmer switch inside him that had been set to low for so long had been turned back up. Now we were moving back to the Dinkley family house next to the Haunted Village. Back where we belonged.

I asked Mom if she'd seen Jinkies that morning, or possibly overnight. "Can you ask Dad?" I prompted her when she said no. Through the phone, I heard his response ("No, why?"), and my stomach dropped.

"We'll find her, honey," my mom promised. "I'm sure she's in one of the boxes."

Yeah, that was kind of what I was afraid of. Poor little Jinkies, trapped! As I ended the call, I reminded myself she was probably fine. Jinkies, like most cats, liked to tuck herself into tiny spaces to test out her sleek moves.

"Okay, Jinkies, you win," I said. "I'm leaving now. I'll be back to find you later!"

I grabbed my messenger bag, laced up my boots, and bounded down the stairs. I'd been thinking all night about the jewels. And about Shaggy. And about the Vanished, and Milford, and Mr. Rogers's face when Shaggy had been talking to the crowd. I had a lot to go over with Daphne.

I found her downtown. (To be clear, her location wasn't a surprise. I'm good at solving mysteries, but Daphne's love of coffee is well known. Plus, she'd posted a photo that showed her in front of The Mocha.)

What *was* a surprise was who she was with: Ram.

Their heads were bent over their notebooks, and they were whispering. They both looked up in surprise when I dropped my bag onto the table and slid into the remaining seat. I almost whistled. Up close, Ram was even more striking. In fact, I realized, he was almost as pretty as Daphne.

"Vel-Velma!" Daphne stuttered. "Hi . . . um, hi!"

"Maybe cut back on the caf, Daph?" I smiled. Then I stuck my hand out to Ram. "Hi. I'm Velma."

He shook it. "Hey. Ram. We work together."

"Got it," I confirmed. Then, for reasons I couldn't quite articulate in the moment, I added, "I've known Daphne pretty much forever." I left out the part about how we hadn't spoken for half that time.

"Cool." He nodded. He glanced back and forth between us. "So . . . what, eighteen years?"

"Actually, we're only sixteen," I corrected him, ignoring Daphne's kick from under the table. Well, who can blame me? He was clearly interested in Daphne, and she was obviously—like, super obviously, based on the pink splotches forming on her otherwise flawless face—into him. But he was in college, and I needed to make sure he was aware that *we* were only in high school.

"Ah," he said, flipping a page in his notebook. Daphne was slowly turning the color of her purple tank top.

Maybe I'd gone too far. I hurriedly tried to change the

subject. "What are you guys doing downtown? I thought you were working this morning, Daph."

"We are." She gestured pointedly to her notebook.

"Oh," I said. It was dawning on me that maybe I was interrupting. See, this was why I wasn't cut out for socializing. "Um, I'll just . . ."

"Actually, I was on my way out," Ram said, gathering his things. He hopped up. "The matinee is letting out in a minute, so it's the perfect time to hit the movie theater. Let's connect back at the office in an hour?"

"Sounds good," Daphne said coolly. She wore the neutral Daphne mask I'd grown used to in the years we hadn't spoken; it was so familiar I began to feel pinpricks of sweat form at the back of my neck. This face was classic Daphne—the one who didn't speak to me, who was mean and cold and thought she was better than everyone. She blankly concentrated on her notebook until we heard the ding of The Mocha's door closing.

"Velma," she hissed, her face relaxing into what I now knew was her real expression, full of emotion. "What is wrong with you?"

"Sorry," I mumbled, even though I wasn't quite sure what I was sorry *for*.

She shook her head and then, in a brief moment of spectacular un-Daphne-like behavior, rested her head on her hands, closed her eyes, and took a deep breath.

"Um," I said. "Are you okay?"

She hesitated, then nodded. When she met my eyes, she was Daphne again—glowing skin, clear eyes, can't lose. "It's just . . . Ram is so much more experienced at this stuff than me. I don't want anyone to think I didn't earn this internship, especially him. Milford really respects him. And everyone already thinks I just get everything handed to me . . ."

Ah. I understood now. Daphne Blake, *the* Daphne Blake, seemed to have it all: the perfect face, the best clothes, the biggest house, the famous mother, the good grades, the popularity. She was always fighting the perception that things came easy for her; that she didn't have to work for anything. That her life was smooth sailing.

I knew better, but even I forgot sometimes. She was just so good at hiding the hard parts, at keeping any emotion, positive or negative, locked up inside. The assumptions people made about me were pretty much the opposite of the ones they made about Daphne, but for some reason—maybe for precisely that reason—that meant we understood each other.

"Daphne, you deserve this internship."

"I know I do. I just want my work to speak for itself." She cleared her throat, sat up straighter, and finished off her coffee with one final sip. "So. What's up? You look like something's bothering you."

She knew me too well. I sighed. "Probably nothing. I

just couldn't find Jinkies this morning. And I looked everywhere."

Daphne tsked. "She probably got stuck in a box somewhere."

"That's what I'm afraid of!" I paused. "Actually, no, *that's* not what I'm afraid of. I'm more worried she took off somehow, maybe snuck out again."

"I'll help you look for her," Daphne offered. "Once Ram and I file this piece, I'm off the clock."

I eyed her notebook. "So what's the piece?"

She smiled. "I'm surprised you haven't heard. I mean, it's not secret—it's all over town."

She filled me in on the police blotter, on all the reports that had come in overnight—plus several new ones this morning—and updated me on the interviews she and Ram had conducted so far. With every update, my heart pounded harder. I pushed back my glasses—I'd ordered contacts last night—and practically fell over in my chair, I was so eager.

"Listen to some of these quotes," Daphne said, flipping pages in her book. "One woman said, 'There are so many terrifying things happening now that I think Crystal Cove should issue a town-wide curfew!' And then one guy told me, 'Wherever those jewels are from, they need to go back. We don't want 'em here.' Then I ran into Trey in front of the skate park, and he said, and I quote, 'I can't wait to get out of this bleeping haunted town.'"

VELMA

"I take it he didn't use the word *bleeping*?"

"It's not funny, Velma." Daphne sighed. "I've never seen this before. People are freaked out!"

"But that's what I came to tell you," I said. "People don't need to be freaked out! Do you remember that one day, the summer we were around seven or eight, and I got that really bad sunburn?"

Daphne threw her hands up in the air. "And this is relevant how?"

"Just hear me out. We had been at the lake all day," I prompted. Near the east end of Crystal Cove, under the mountains, were some stunning lakes and rivers that were crowded with people year-round. My mom, who was a little afraid of sea creatures, much preferred the lakes to the beach, and we often spent summer days out there.

She sighed and then nodded, thinking. "Yeah, I remember. We had put on sunscreen but then . . ."

"Then we got so busy, I forgot to reapply," I confirmed. "Do you remember what we were so busy doing?"

Daphne squinted. For a second, she looked just like she had as a little kid, her face open, real. She snapped her fingers. "My earrings!"

"Exactly!" I slapped the table in triumph. The people at the table next to us glared. "Sorry," I told them hastily before dropping my voice. "You'd lost one of your topaz earrings somewhere on that beach. We spent hours looking for it."

"So?"

"So, do you remember where we eventually found it?"

Daphne nodded and flicked a lock of her hair off her shoulder. She was wearing a purple headband I'd never seen before. I just knew that, by the following week, everyone at school would be wearing headbands. "Yes! It was over by the canoes, right near the shore." She shook her head. "That was so lucky. I still can't believe we found it."

"Right. Sitting at the bottom of a pool of water." I stressed the word *bottom*, and then, for good measure, repeated it. "*Bottom.*"

"Velma."

"Okay, okay," I relented. "The earring was at the bottom of the lake because topazes are heavier than water. Denser. They sink."

"And . . ." Daphne's voice trailed off.

"And once I remembered that topazes sink in water, I researched other jewels. Like all the ones that washed up."

Daphne smiled. "Let me guess. They sink in water, too."

"Yep!" I mimed applause.

"But yesterday, on the beach . . ."

"The washed-up jewels were floating!"

Daphne's eyes flashed. "Which means . . ."

"It means," I said, thinking of the way the jewels had floated on top of the waves, brushing against our knees as we stood in the sea, "it means those jewels aren't real."

The old man bends over his work, steam fogging up his glasses. He pushes and presses and tugs, trying to smooth out the fabric. Classical music plays from the old radio under the counter and he hums along to it mindlessly.

Ding.

He doesn't look up from his work, but he does call out a hearty, "Welcome!" Any fool could see he's busy, and besides, his customers are regulars, and they know he'll be with them as soon as he can.

It takes another minute for him to straighten up, his lower back screaming at him. He remembers when he used to be a young man, hearty and full of jumpy energy that made it impossible for him to sit still. He longs for a bit of that feeling these days.

He pushes through a rack of clothes, a smile on his face. Maybe it's old Caroline Stine, who drops off her business suits every week like clockwork. Seventy years old and still working full-time at the bank, that Caroline. He knows a few youngsters who could take a page from her playbook. Plus, Caroline usually has the best stories. She knows everyone in town . . . including how much money they have, or don't have, as the case often is.

But the front of the store is empty. "Hello?" he calls, just in case. But it's silly; there's nowhere to hide. Just two folding chairs in front of the large storefront window make up his waiting room.

Oh well. He must be hearing things. He shrugs and walks back to his spot behind the counter, past the racks. He'll get the latest scoop from her next time.

Hiss, says his steamer.

Back to work, his mind wanders. It's been doing that a lot these days. Who is he to make fun of old Caroline Stine? he wonders. He's pushing seventy himself, even though his back makes him feel more like ninety.

Yes, seventy years here in Crystal Cove. He's seen it all— the good, the bad, the changes. The hauntings, the ghosts, the stories. He's been in this place long enough to know what's real and what's just a juicy story.

And he likes the juicy stories—can't blame him there! He chuckles to himself, thinking of a particularly scandalous one the mechanic down the street told him. His laugh fades when he realizes the steady beeping he thought was coming from the radio is actually coming from the front of the store.

Huffing, he walks up front, brushing aside the same rack of clothes. The beeping is loud, incessant. It's the register.

His son made him buy one of those newfangled ones, and now it's beeping and whining at him. He can't hear himself think. He taps and pushes, but it doesn't quiet down until he unplugs the thing.

He tries to catch his breath, wondering why on earth the register went crazy. The doorbell, too.

He scans the store. For a moment, he even considers ducking under the counter just to check that it's clear. He steps over to the front window and looks outside, up and down the block. It's midafternoon, that time of day when everyone's at work or taking a siesta or catching a matinee or a late lunch. Why can't he shake this feeling, then, that someone is here with him? Watching him?

It's the stories, he realizes. Those silly stories everyone's talking about all around town are freaking him out. Old ladies this and mysterious noises that, and on and on they go, as if everyone is suddenly willing to believe every rumor about Crystal Cove's supposedly haunted past is true.

He harrumphs and hobbles back to his station, steam rising from his tools, all the colors of the rainbow and then some jumbled around the workshop.

But a few minutes into his steaming and, click, *the radio goes dead.*

He freezes. Has the electricity in his whole store gone haywire?

A sudden, loud burst of static from the speakers makes him jump, kicking over the ironing board. Hisssssss, *cries the steamer. He frantically picks it up before it ruins the floors.*

Perhaps it's time for a break.

He sits on the stool behind the now-dead register, sipping at a cup of tea. He crosses his arms, staring at nothing, thinking about what old Caroline Stine said that very morning when she dropped off her suits.

"I can't go into specifics," she said—Caroline could never go into specifics, which was what made her stories so maddeningly believable—as a look of genuine fear had flashed in her eyes. "But we've had a few clients pull their investments because of these awful circumstances."

"What circumstances?" he asked, baffled. But Caroline just shook her head.

"You know," she whispered, leaning in over the counter. He caught a whiff of her perfume, strong and floral and mature. "The hauntings."

He laughed her off then. But now, sitting in his shop, even in the broad daylight? It suddenly all seems a little too real.

He knows what to do, he realizes. He'll talk to all the neighbors, compare stories. They'll get a kick out of the strange electronic disturbances he's had today, that's for sure.

Yes, if there's one thing he knows, it's that everyone loves a good story. Even more so when it's a spooky one.

He flips the sign on his door from OPEN to BACK IN A FEW MINUTES and pulls on his jacket. Suddenly, he hears a rustling in the back, behind the clothes racks. He pauses.

There it is again.

"Who's there?" he demands. But no one answers.

Of course not, he tells himself. No one else is here.

Quickly, he opens the door and steps outside.

He's been in Crystal Cove long enough to know what's real and what's just a rumor.

How strange it is, though, that for the first time he can remember, some of these rumors are starting to feel a little too real.

DAPHNE

"EXCELLENT!"

Ram flashed a grin my way. At his desk in front of us, flipping through the printout we'd just given him, Milford Jones was jubilant.

"Truly an outstanding piece of reporting!" He nodded, satisfaction blooming on his face. "I'll certainly take some credit here. You two make a good reporting team. It was smart of me to pair you two together!"

What I wanted to do was keel over and beg the floor to swallow me up. What I actually did was fight back a blush, call up my neutral Daphne mask, and thank Milford for the compliment. Next to me, Ram did the same, and we hurried back to our seats when Milford dismissed us.

"That guy," Ram said, shaking his head.

DAPHNE

"I know. But at least he loved our piece!"

If I did say so myself, our story on how the townspeople of Crystal Cove felt about the jewels washing ashore—or, more accurately, about the rumors about where the jewels had come from—felt super professional. The quotes Ram and I had taken from a diverse range of residents showed a breadth of opinions that, I think, represented Crystal Cove perfectly. The good, the bad, and the spooky.

For example, old Rosamund Brooks talked my ear off about how she'd had a recurring dream her whole life about the Vanished returning, all bones and sagging skin, rotted teeth and wispy clothes, and didn't I think that was prophetic? (Gross? Yes. Prophetic? No.)

But Ram, the poor guy, had it worse. When he'd left me and Velma, he'd hit up the movie theater, and the matinee had just ended. In a stroke of bad luck, the only movie playing in town was that new blockbuster about a jewel heist gone wrong. He'd been practically overrun with townspeople wanting to get their names in the *Howler*, and they had even wilder and weirder conspiracy theories than any of the folks I'd interviewed. One person suggested the jewels came from an ancient race of aliens who'd crashed into the sea and were unable to escape to their home planet; another demanded to get Milford's number so he could "call the media and get personal updates on the case."

But that was the thing: There wasn't really a case. At least, not yet. My sources at the *Howler* said Lieutenant Rogers was dedicating very limited resources to figuring this whole thing out, due to the fact that there were no victims. No reported thefts, no injuries. Just . . . a mystery.

An even more confusing one, now that I knew the jewels were fake.

Ram grabbed his backpack and slipped his headphones over his neck. "I gotta run."

I nodded. "Me too." While I'd been busy filing our piece, I'd noticed Velma had texted a couple times. My fingers itched to see what she wanted. Probably, I realized with a wince, to know when Milford was going to publish the news she'd discovered. She'd even texted me a sample headline: **TOWN REALIZES JEWELS ARE FAKE; WHEN WILL THEY REALIZE MILFORD JONES IS, TOO?**

Obviously, she was joking. (But at the same time . . . kind of serious.)

It was all irrelevant, anyway, because I hadn't told Milford yet. I hadn't told *anybody* yet, not even Ram. Partly because as an intern, I doubted anyone would take me seriously. Partly because I still couldn't think of a reason *why* someone would go to the trouble of dumping fake jewels in the sea, and that felt like a crucial part of my reporting.

And partly because I had really enjoyed the day I'd spent with Ram . . . and, selfishly, I worried Milford would reassign us to different cases once the solution of the jewel case finally came to light.

Truly, I'm a terrible person. But, I reminded myself grimly, I was working on it.

"Doing anything cool?" Ram continued, hoisting up one of his orange-sneaker-clad feet and retying his laces.

"That depends on whether Velma needs me," I said, gesturing to my phone, which lit up with yet another text, as if on command. We both laughed. "And honestly, I'm kind of afraid to find out."

Ram had switched feet now. "You two are close."

"Now? Yeah. We are." Inside, I was giddy. The fact that he noticed felt important, somehow. Like he was observing. Not in a creepy way, just in a nice way. I hadn't had a guy pay attention to me in a while. Maybe ever. Not like this, anyway. And that's the thing a lot of guys didn't realize about dating me: I didn't want compliments, or flowers, or fancy dinners, or revved-up cars. I just wanted to be heard. To be understood. I wanted a guy who saw not just what was important to me, but *who* was important. A guy who was good with me having a best friend, especially one like Velma—someone with her own unflappable mind. Someone I shared a history with, and also a whole lot of conflict . . . but also a ton of laughs. We were layered, me and Velma. And right now, we were a package deal.

I guess I could just chalk it up to Ram being a journalist.

But it was nice to think it was more than that. To think it was about *me*.

"Like some kind of crime-fighting duo." He shot me his warmest smile. I'd mentioned in passing that Velma and I had a knack for figuring things out, and I tried not to blush.

"You have no idea," I confirmed.

"You should probably get that." He pointed. I jumped. My phone was ringing. Velma.

"I'll see you later," I called, tapping my screen. Ram waved and jogged out around our cubicle corner, down the hall, and to the elevators.

"What's up, V?"

"Daph! Haven't you been getting my texts?"

"I was working. But we just filed our story, so I'm done now. What's going on?"

There was a pause, and then Velma's voice, sounding shaky. "It's Jinkies."

* * *

I hadn't been in Velma's apartment since before my stepdad had unearthed the deed to the Dinkleys' original land. It was rough going in there, overcrowded and dark, and the low ceilings combined with the miserable look on Velma's face only made it worse. I patted her shoulder while she tried to pull herself together.

We were at the kitchen table. I'd brought over some

DAPHNE

chocolate chip cookies from Velma's favorite bakery—it was on my way, and I'd thought they'd make her feel better—but they sat untouched in front of us.

"I thought she'd be back by now!" Velma said, sniffling.

I made her go over the whole thing with me again. It was the only thing I could think to do. She sighed and sort of slumped over, but then repeated it all to me. Again.

Jinkies always slept in Velma's bed, except for occasional nights when something would spook her and she'd dart away, usually under her parents' bed. But even then, by morning, she'd slink back into Velma's room, her purrs acting as Velma's daily alarm.

Jinkies was an indoor cat but, like all creatures, she occasionally attempted a getaway. The window in the kitchen was usually the culprit, because Velma's mom liked to keep it open whenever she cooked, and the screen behind it wasn't super reliable. (Velma's mom's cooking was legendary. My mouth watered whenever Velma mentioned it.)

As Velma started to go down the dangerous path of explaining, in meticulous detail, what kinds of food her mom liked to cook—chilaquiles and enchiladas and pozole—I quickly shepherded her back to the important details. Namely, what had happened that morning.

"Jinkies disappeared sometime in the middle of the night," she explained. She covered her face with her hands.

"Sorry, I don't mean to be so emotional about this."

I almost snorted. "You've seen me be emotional plenty of times. Don't worry about it. Just tell me what happened."

She nodded. "I was still sleeping when my parents left. They went to breakfast, but they swear they didn't see her at all before they left. And when I woke up, she was just . . . gone."

"And you checked everywhere?" I prompted. When she nodded, I pressed harder. "Every closet? Every box?"

"There are only two closets in this crummy place. Three if you count my 'bedroom.'" She made air quotes around *bedroom*.

She continued, "As for the boxes . . . well, I checked most of them. All the open ones, anyway. I'm assuming Jinkies can't magically break into a sealed-up box, but maybe I'm wrong?"

Velma looked so hopeful in that moment that I didn't want to crush her. "Maybe!"

Her face fell. "Will you come with me to search the neighborhood?"

I opened my tote and pulled out the reason I'd been so late getting to Velma's: a stack of MISSING CAT flyers, complete with a large color photo of Jinkies and both our phone numbers. I'd printed them out at the *Howler* offices. "Of course. And I brought provisions."

DAPHNE

In a completely uncharacteristic move, Velma leaned over and wrapped both arms around my neck.

"Sheesh," I grumbled. But little bursts of warmth were popping inside my chest.

* * *

It was dusk by the time we papered the last of the flyers onto the bulletin board inside the dry cleaner's around the block from Velma's apartment. We'd been everywhere we could think of in her neighborhood—the bougie gym that had recently opened, the post office, the two car-repair shops that were situated across the street from each other and had spawned generations of competition. I'd done most of the actual posting, and the pads of my fingers were raw from pressing so many pushpins into so many bulletin boards; Velma had spent most of the afternoon calling for Jinkies, checking in with her parents to see if she'd come home yet, and ducking inside every alleyway we passed and under nearly every parked car on the street.

I was exhausted.

Frank, the dry cleaner, read our flyer with interest. "Poor Jinkies!" he said, whiffs of steam from one of his irons puffing into the air behind him. "Sweet little cat."

"Have you seen her today?" Velma asked hopefully.

Frank shook his head, his eyes darting through the big shop window and out to the darkening street. "I'm trying to keep to myself these days."

I frowned. Frank was infamous in Crystal Cove for his love of gossip. If you needed to know something about a neighbor, you came to him. "What do you mean?"

"You know the jewels?" Frank's voice dropped. "The *ghost jewels*?"

Velma and I glanced at each other. I was trying to convey a message to her—an oh-no-has-Frank-lost-it kind of message—and I think she was broadcasting the same to me. But honestly, that's the problem with glances. No one can ever really be sure their message is being correctly interpreted.

"The . . . ghost jewels?" Velma repeated. "The ones that washed up yesterday?"

"Not a good omen," Frank whispered. Outside, the sun slipped behind the row of buildings across the street, casting a shadow through the store. Suddenly, one of Frank's machines hissed. I jumped and absolutely hated myself for it.

"The jewels have nothing to do with omens," I countered.

"Or ghosts," Velma said pointedly. I could sense her diminishing patience more than hear it—she shuffled her boots on the floor and tucked her brown hair behind her ears. Then she cleared her throat, twice—a signal to me that it was time to get going. We were out of flyers, anyway.

"You girls don't get it," said Frank, shaking his head. "It

DAPHNE

doesn't matter whether they're really ghost jewels or not. It's all what people believe. And people believe they belong to the Vanished."

"Is that what you've been hearing today?" I asked him.

He nodded. "At first I didn't believe it myself. But my customers keep telling me about the strange things they saw last night. Things that can't be explained. And when people can't explain things, they start doing weird things. Acting irrationally. Like keeping their kids home from Sunday school, or withdrawing their life savings from the bank . . ." His voice trailed off. "The power of suggestion is just that . . . powerful."

Velma stared at him thoughtfully. "Have you seen anything weird yourself? Or just heard spooky stories from customers?"

He shrugged. "I'm not usually one to believe in ghost stories, but I'd be lying if I said I hadn't been a bit spooked today." A funny look came over his face, but he shook it off. "Anyway. I hope your missing kitty isn't part of the strange events going on in town. I'll keep an eye out for her."

"We appreciate that. Thanks again for letting us post this here," I said, my voice smooth, hiding the reaction I really wanted to share. (Which was, to be clear, rolling my eyes. I couldn't believe yet another adult thought ghosts were roaming the streets.)

Once we were safely out of Frank's eyesight, we plopped

down on the bench outside the corner store without a word. I asked Velma what she thought of old Frank.

"He's usually harmless," she said doubtfully, staring blankly across the street. "But I agree it's . . . well, unfortunate that he's acting all creeped out now."

"He's always been a busybody," I confirmed.

"But it's not great that the town gossip believes the jewels are bad luck. People tell him stuff, and they listen to him," Velma said. "And he's right about one thing: People do weird things when they're scared."

"Yeah," I agreed. I thought of the many people I'd interviewed that day, and how most of them were on edge about the whole thing. Having someone like Frank spreading scary stories . . . well, it was like lighting a spark at a gas station. Dangerous, fast, and stupid.

Velma sighed. "Jinkies?" This time her call was half-hearted, like she was about to give up.

"Any word from your parents?" I wondered.

"My mom just texted a few minutes ago. No sign of her yet."

Hmm. If I were Jinkies, where would I be? I considered her options while we sat in silence. Suddenly, I had an idea. I straightened up, feeling positive for the first time since we'd begun this cat hunt.

"You guys have been prepping your new house—I mean, your old house—for the move, right?" I asked. I knew it was true, that Velma and her parents had made several trips to their new house, which was really their old house, since the deed had been recovered.

"Yeah, at least one of us stops by every day. There's a lot to do to get it ready."

"And Jinkies lived in that house before you moved into your apartment?"

Velma nodded. I paused, letting the idea come to her in its own time. Velma liked to have the answers, and sometimes I liked to lead her right to them. It was a win-win: I had the satisfaction of knowing I'd come up with the solution, but Velma got to actually voice it out loud.

". . . And I've brought him to the new house almost every time I've been there this past week!" She jumped up. "Daphne, you're a genius!"

* * *

The new-old Dinkley house sat on a large plot of land on the outskirts of Crystal Cove's downtown. I spent a lot of time here as a kid, running around the history museum Velma's parents ran and playing hide-and-seek in the rambling Victorian house they lived in just next door. But when our friendship blew up, so did this land— metaphorically, at least. The town sold the history museum, plus the land it lived on . . . which meant the Dinkleys had to vacate their house.

When the museum was sold, this place became a giant,

cheesy tourist trap, capitalizing on the success of my mom's video game and drawing all sorts of ghost-hungry crowds. Plastic, mildly scary souvenirs littered the new storefronts here; the night sky lit up from the neon Ferris wheel and roller coaster, and canned screams from the haunted house echoed through the park. I admit it was kind of a fun place to go when I reached the age where my dad would let me hang out, unsupervised, with my friends, but I knew Velma had nothing but bad memories of the Haunted Village.

But all's well that ends well, I guess, because Velma's father was proven right when the land's original deed was finally uncovered. And now the Dinkleys were moving back into the house; they were busy making plans for how to transform the space into something they could be proud of. Knowing Velma's mom, who didn't like anything in Crystal Cove to change much, I wouldn't be surprised if she reverted these buildings back to some kind of walking tour of history. But it was unclear if Mr. Rogers, who held more influence in this town than any other single person, would go for that.

We plodded across the open field that led up to the house's backyard, the moonlight—and our memories—guiding our way. It was quiet now that the Haunted Village was closed, and the darkened buildings stood empty against the night sky, giving the whole place an air of abandonment. My stomach growled, puncturing the silence.

DAPHNE

"Let's order Chinese after this," Velma offered.

She fished a set of keys out of her messenger bag as we approached the back door. A single light bulb hung directly over our heads, casting funny shadows over our faces. I shivered. The temperature had dropped significantly since the sun set.

Click. Velma turned the lock and the knob, and the door creaked open.

"When's the last time that door was used?" I joked, but nervously, because the door really did seem like it was too fragile to perform its intended function. Strips of it had peeled off; they hung dangerously from its center pane.

"My dad's been sanding a replacement." Velma pointed to the far corner of the kitchen, where we'd come in, I squinted in the weak light and noticed a makeshift workshop set up, with a large door resting on cinder blocks.

I cautiously stepped inside. The Dinkleys had never had a ton of money, but life in this house had been comfortable; cozy. Now that this place had been sitting empty for several years, I could see how much work had to be done to get it in shape for move-in day.

"When are you moving in again?" I asked, running my finger over a thick layer of dust on the kitchen counter.

"Whenever it's ready." Velma's voice was muffled; I whirled around to find she was crouching inside the cabinets under the sink, aiming her phone's flashlight inside. "Jinkies!"

I whistled. *Ready* was relative, I guess. I flicked on my flashlight. "I'll take the living room?"

"Okay!" Half her body was now fully inside the cabinet.

I stepped through the swinging kitchen door—these old Victorians were the opposite of the sprawling, open-concept Blake house—chuckling a little at the image of Velma's butt under the kitchen sink. Then I stopped. "Jinkies?" I whispered, alarmed to hear the shakiness in my own voice.

Either a tornado had hit the living room, or the Dinkleys were really packing up their apartment way too soon, because the place was an unmitigated disaster. It was nowhere near ready for them to move in. Odd, broken pieces of furniture dotted the room—a single armchair under one of the windows, its stuffing now falling out of rips and tears in its faded fabric; two end tables, each with broken legs that made the tables slope to one side. Even the front windows were broken, with ragged cracks cutting across the panes like lightning bolts.

Plus, it was dark in there. Really, really dark.

I'm not afraid of the dark, and I'm definitely not afraid of "ghosts." And while I don't love cats, I liked Jinkies well enough, and I certainly wasn't worried she'd pop out of some hidden, secret place and give me a heart attack.

No, what set fear into my heart was the notion that someone—namely, the Dinkleys—would have to do a massive amount of work to get this place into order. And I didn't see how anything short of a bulldozer would accomplish that.

I ventured cautiously into the living room, searching under the furniture and behind the random items someone had left on the mantel. Finally, following the trail of footprints (which I hoped were paw prints from a cat, and not some other unwelcome creature) through the dust on the floorboards and up the staircase, I called out to Velma that I was headed upstairs. She didn't answer. I reached out to hold the handrail, then thought better of it.

"Jinkies! Here, kitty, kitty!"

The second floor was, somehow, darker than the first. I tiptoed down the hallway, calling Jinkies's name and cursing my phone's flashlight function, which cast a shockingly weak light up here in the pitch-black.

I stopped by Velma's old room first and slowly opened the door, calling Jinkies's name. I was surprised by what I found inside—or rather, what I didn't find: a mess. Velma's room was clean, the floors and windows gleaming, and free of junky furniture. I squinted at the wall and smiled. The room was completely bare except for some framed photos she'd already hung next to the window that overlooked the front yard. One of them was an old picture of the two of us dressed for Halloween. We were about six or seven, and I was in the biggest, pinkest princess gown my mom could find. Velma, her face hidden in a helmet, was an astronaut. In the photo, we're gripping each other's hands and grinning at the camera. Or at least, I assumed Velma was grinning. It was hard to tell.

I couldn't help it—I squealed out loud, breaking the silence surrounding me. I had hidden all the photos of me and Velma after that awful time when we stopped speaking and, even though we had mended things, I hadn't yet unearthed them from the old boxes in my closet. My stomach knotted as I looked at the tiny versions of us. Those girls—they were so sweet, so earnest. They had so much to learn.

"Psst! Jinkies!" I slid open the closet door. Nothing.

I whirled around, deciding on my next move. The northeast-facing window in Velma's room caught my attention, and I strode over and peered out of it. There were no blinds or curtains on it yet, giving me a broad view of the old Haunted Village. I'd never seen it from this perspective, and it struck me then just how big and foreboding it all looked, especially now that it was empty.

But it was peaceful, too, in a way. I let my mind wander while my eyes roamed. The Haunted Village had been tacky and silly, sure, but it had also helped drive sales of my mom's video game, further cementing her—our?—fame and fortune. Sometimes it was still hard to fathom the full legacy my mom's work had left on the world; the imprint of it in Crystal Cove's history. I began to get lost in my thoughts—about my mom and what we'd been through, about what it feels like to be a part of a famous town's foundation, and how both Velma and I could say that—until a blur of orange caught my eye.

My breath caught in my throat as I leaned closer, my forehead nearly touching the glass. There it was again—a streak of color in an otherwise-gray landscape, gone almost as soon as I registered it.

My senses went on full alert as I willed my eyes to stay focused. The Haunted Village was still dark, still empty. From my second-floor perch, I peered at the town's windows and corners, straining to see into the darkest shadows. Waiting.

I gasped out loud when I saw it again. Now it was a fiery red color, stark against the gray buildings, and it lingered just enough for my eyes to adjust to its presence, for my mind to try to make sense of it.

But it couldn't be. It *couldn't*. I shook my head, murmuring a denial into Velma's empty bedroom.

The fiery streak paused in front of a small cluster of birch trees outside what used to be the candy store and then, almost as if it knew I was upstairs, watching, it swiveled in a circle until it—I gulped then, desperate for breath—*looked right at me.*

It was a person. A woman.

With long red hair.

Like mine.

I was frozen in place, my feet rooted to the floor, heart seizing with alarm.

Then I blinked, and she was gone.

I hurried out of Velma's room, farther down the hall, racing to find another window. Maybe the woman, or whatever it was, would be visible from a different angle. My heart raced and I told myself to calm down, to breathe. The Haunted Village was technically closed, sure, but that didn't mean people couldn't sneak in. Even though the gates had been locked up tight since its closing . . .

I tried not to think about how, even though *people* would have trouble getting inside, ghosts probably wouldn't.

Out in the hallway were two closed doors: one to the master bedroom, and one to the small, tight staircase that led to the attic. I needed a window fast, and besides, I wasn't psyched about going up to the third and final floor of this house (even as a kid, that staircase had felt too tiny for my little feet to traverse; I'd once slipped on a middle step and tumbled down, landing with a thud at the closed door, and I wasn't eager to risk another fall . . . not in these boots).

DAPHNE

So I turned my attention to the master bedroom. The door, gray and foreboding, beckoned me. For some reason, I felt the need to knock on it, as though I needed to warn someone I was about to enter. "Stupid," I said out loud. But still, I opened the door slowly. Cautiously.

Creaaakkkk.

The room was a black hole. Not a single speck of light could be found. I tapped my screen and shone the flashlight around, noticing that the blinds on all four windows had been pulled tightly down, blocking whatever weak moonlight was shining outside.

Suddenly, without warning, the flashlight flicked off. My phone's battery had died.

"Jinkies?" I half whispered into the darkness, still standing in the door frame. My legs refused to take any further steps.

I was keenly aware of my breath, my heartbeat, the blood coursing through my veins. Every sense my body could perform appeared to be working overtime, like it was on high alert.

I forced my legs to move, one step at a time, until I reached the closest window. I'd left the door open, of course, and my eyes had adjusted just enough to make out the walls around me. This room, too, was empty, as best I could tell. No Jinkies, and no orange flashes, either.

I drew a shaky breath and reached over to the window, pulling up the blinds.

The air around me seemed to reverberate in response. From this window I saw the back half of the Haunted Village—clusters of small buildings, still dark and empty, dotted with trees, their branches sparse enough to let moonlight angle through them and hit the ground, casting odd shadows.

I didn't see the woman, but I still, for some reason, thought I should call out to her. "Hello?"

"Hey," came a voice from behind me, from inside the room.

I screamed.

VELMA

JINKIES WAS NOT UNDER the kitchen sink. She also wasn't in the downstairs bathroom or behind the curtains in the dining room, and I saw no sign of her in the tiny room we called a basement. I crossed my fingers as I bounded up the stairs to find Daphne.

Her footsteps were no longer visible once I hit the second-floor landing; Mom had been spending most of her time up here, getting the bedrooms ready, while Dad did most of the packing back in the apartment, and as a result the floors up here were shiny and clean, free of the dust and inexplicable twigs and leaves littering the staircase. I peeked into my new-old room, the bathroom, and the guest room before noticing Daphne standing in my parents' room, looking like . . . well, like she'd just seen a ghost.

"Hello?" I heard her say as I approached the door.

"Hey," I responded.

I wasn't expecting the scream that followed, nor the way Daphne crumpled over, as though she were fainting.

"Daph! Are you okay?" I cried. I rushed to her side, but first I flipped the switch next to the door. The overhead light flickered on.

Daphne blinked furiously and got to her feet. "What the . . ."

"You're shaking," I noticed. "What happened?"

"I . . . I just . . ." Daphne's face was paler than usual, her skin nearly translucent. She glanced at the overhead light in a way that made me wonder if she'd ever seen electricity before.

A thought occurred to me. "Have you been walking around up here in the dark?"

"You don't have to say it like I'm an idiot!" she wailed. "I thought you guys hadn't turned on the power yet!"

I stared in horror at Daphne for a moment before—and I hate myself for this, truly—bursting into a guffaw.

"You're covered in dust!" I pointed at the gray smudges trailing her arms.

"Why didn't you turn on the lights downstairs when we got here?" Daphne complained. And rightfully so—I was still choking back laughter.

VELMA

I threw up my hands. "I was in a rush to find Jinkies! I don't know!"

Daphne shot me daggers. Ah, I knew that look well. The Daphne of the past few years—pre our making up—had just two expressions in reserve for me: utter disinterest or outright hate. (Of the two, I almost preferred the hate.)

"I'm sorry," I relented. "I guess I should've told you to . . . turn on the lights?"

I could barely get the words out before I started laughing again. I couldn't help it!

"I hate you," Daphne said. "But there's no time for that now. I saw something outside. We have to go look for it."

"What? What do you mean?"

She hesitated. "I *thought* I saw something. This is going to sound crazy, but I think it was the Lady Vampire of the Bay."

I frowned. "In the Village? Probably some random kids. Unless . . ." I paused. "Daphne! This is our chance to find out who's behind all the spooky sightings. We gotta go!"

Together, we hurried down the stairs and out the front door. On the porch, we paused for a minute.

"Where did you see her?" I asked.

"Down the hill, by the old candy store," Daphne said, nodding in that direction.

I pulled my phone out of the pocket of my hoodie and turned on the flashlight function. "Okay. Let's go."

THE DARK DECEPTION

We ran into the Haunted Village, passing Pizza Panic, the place where I used to work, and also the old town jail, where I'd found Daphne's friend Marcy locked up a few months ago. There was no one around.

Daphne was lagging behind me a bit—probably because of the ridiculous high-heeled boots she was wearing. But when I turned around to urge her onward, she had a funny look on her face. Like she was genuinely scared.

"Come on, Daph," I said. "We're almost there. Don't let this place get under your skin."

She nodded. "Over there," she said, pointing at a pair of birch trees by the candy shop. "I saw the figure disappear between those trees."

I cast my flashlight's beam over the pale white branches and beyond. There was no one there. And beyond the trees was the wrought-iron fence that surrounded the whole park.

I pointed my flashlight at the ground. The earth was firm and smooth—it hadn't rained in a few days, so there was no chance of finding footprints. But something else glinted in the flashlight's beam.

Daphne gasped. She'd seen it too. "Velma!"

We stepped closer to the fence. There, next to one of the iron posts, was a gleaming red stone the size of a large pebble.

"It's a ruby," Daphne breathed. She pulled a tissue out of

her pocket and carefully used it to pick up the stone. It was bright and clean—it couldn't've been there long.

"Someone was here," I said slowly. A cold finger of fear seemed to run down my spine. I usually prided myself on being logical, but standing in the Haunted Village, looking down at the stone in my friend's hand, I couldn't help feeling spooked.

"Do you think it was really the Lady Vampire?" Daphne asked, tearing her eyes off the stone to look at me searchingly.

I took a deep breath and shook my head, feeling like myself again. "No. But someone wants us to think it is."

* * *

I'm almost ashamed to admit it, but Daphne and I held hands as we walked back up the hill toward my house. We'd looked around for a few more minutes, but there was no other sign of the Lady Vampire, or the person impersonating her. Together we checked the doors of the stands and shops near the candy store, but they were all tightly locked. Whoever Daphne had seen, whoever had left behind the stone . . . whoever it was, they were gone.

Now the stone was wrapped in a tissue in my hoodie pocket. We'd decided we should bring it to Burnett's to ask Noelle to take a look.

I took a deep breath as we climbed the back porch steps.

THE DARK DECEPTION

Right now, I wanted nothing more than to go back to my shoebox-like apartment and curl up in bed. But we still had Jinkies to think of.

Daphne looked over at me. "I know, I want to go home, too. But we gotta find Jinkies," I said.

She nodded wearily. Then she straightened up, as if she'd heard something. "V, did you hear that?"

"What?" I asked.

"Behind you!" Daphne rushed over to a small half-door hidden tucked in the corner of the porch. My mom used to store gardening equipment there... along with extra bags of cat food.

Daphne gave the door a light kick with one booted foot—the door always used to stick. Then she popped it open . . . and a tentative pink nose popped out.

"Jinkies!" I cried. My beloved cat was covered in a fine layer of grime, but she was here. She was found.

"You poor little kitty," I cooed, scooping her up and kissing the tip of her nose.

At last, we could go home. We took a final lap through the house, turning off lights and putting back what we'd pulled out, and then, holding tight to Jinkies, I locked the kitchen door behind us. I glanced at the little half closet at the other end of the back porch. The wood of that old lattice door swelled in the rain and heat, which had always made it tricky to open and close. It was easy to imagine how a cat could wander in there and get trapped.

* * *

On Monday morning, after the requisite snuggling with Jinkies, I did the unthinkable: I texted Shaggy Rogers.

Everyone knew Shaggy Rogers hated text messages. And phones. And technology of any kind. I had personally witnessed his anti-technology stance evolve from its early stages; as kids, whenever Fred Jones would show off all his latest gadgets—not just phones but also video game consoles and MP3 players and Bluetooth speakers—Shaggy would roll his eyes and play fetch with Scooby instead, or take him for a walk, or ditch us all and go surfing. Back then, his mom used to ground him not because he used his cell phone too much, but because he didn't use it enough— he'd go out and leave it at home, so she'd have no way to reach him.

Still. These days he had a phone—*everyone* had a phone—and I had it on good authority that Shaggy's mom insisted he bring it with him to school every day. As a lieutenant, she was hyper focused on safety and demanded her only son be easily reachable in case of an emergency.

As a result, everyone knew Shaggy's number. But everyone also knew not to use it. There was no point; he'd rarely answer it.

I'd fallen asleep thinking about the mystery of the jewels—especially the new jewel we'd found—and Shaggy in equal parts. Usually my best thinking happens early in the morning—I once got an A on a term paper that I didn't start writing until five a.m. the day it was due—but that night, two ideas came to me just as drowsiness hit. So instead of sleeping, I popped out of bed to organize my thoughts and jot down my plans for the next morning.

At what I hoped was an appropriate hour in the morning, I texted Shaggy: **Meet me at The Mocha before school? Breakfast on me!**

Was I going for bribery by mentioning breakfast? Yes. Did I think it would work? Also yes.

I found my mom in the kitchen, sipping coffee and flipping through the *Howler*. I'd heard about this special weekday edition from Daphne; Milford had published a supplement that was filled entirely with content about the washed-up jewels, along with healthy doses of rumors and legends about Crystal Cove's peculiar past. I rolled my eyes at the cover image—a sketch of what I guessed was supposed to be the Lady Vampire of the Bay—as my mom studied its pages.

"Where's Dad?" I grumbled. The thought of sleazy Milford Jones once again capitalizing on Crystal Cove's past—the hypocrite who hated Elizabeth Blake for supposedly doing the same thing—had apparently turned my morning ambition into straight-up grumpiness.

My mom sipped and sighed. "He's still sleeping, mi amor."

She left words unspoken: It was one of *those* days for my dad, which meant he might not make it out of bed today. I tried not to let the news affect me, but it was hard. He'd had a solid few weeks, but I knew, at least logically, that his progress wouldn't be linear. Still. It just set the tone for the day.

As I toasted some bread and searched for the peanut butter, my mom clicked her tongue, muttering.

"I don't know why you read that trash," I said over the ding of the toaster. "It just makes you mad."

"I need to know what people are saying," my mom said with a shrug. "Besides, these kinds of stories are all part of the character of this town."

My mother had a knack not just for talking to people with different beliefs and priorities than she had, but also for making them feel heard. It's why she was so successful at community organizing, how she'd managed to get the town to agree to require certain stipulations in all dealings with real estate developers and local businesses. It's why she had a list of friends and contacts, people who would drop everything and do her a favor, whenever she called.

Unlike me, her bull-in-a-china-shop of a daughter. I was

either too direct, too bold . . . or completely invisible and meaningless. It just depended on who you were asking.

"And what are the fine people of Crystal Cove scared of this morning?" I asked sarcastically. Despite what Daphne and I had found the night before—or maybe because of it—this morning the gullibility of the town seemed extra outrageous to me.

"Velma. Dinkley."

I froze. Uh-oh.

"I want you to listen to me carefully."

I dropped my toast, wiped the crumbs off my palms, and trudged to the table. I couldn't meet my mom's eyes yet. No one likes a heaping dose of disappointment before they've eaten breakfast.

My mom, champion of the picket sign, defender of Crystal Cove history, placed one of her hands on mine.

"Velma. From almost the moment you were born, you were obsessed with science. You mastered puzzles before you could walk."

I expected anger, or at least sternness, when she spoke, but her voice was gentle. Instructive.

"You demanded games that involved logic and reason and shunned all the fairy-tale magical stuff so many adults try to shove onto girls. Your brain is wired to look for evidence, to ground stories in science. And I love that about you!"

VELMA

I blinked. There was a *but* coming, and I could tell it was going to be a big one.

"But."

I let myself smile, but quickly erased it at the serious look on my mom's face.

"The people of Crystal Cove have been through a lot. You might have noticed, some weird stuff happens here on occasion," she went on. "It's fine to be doubtful. It's even fine to encourage people to question their biases, to trust that science has all the answers. I would expect nothing less from you."

It was rare that my mom went into full-on lecture mode. I braced myself.

"But everyone deserves our respect," my mother continued. "Even the people who believe in curses, or hauntings, or any number of unexplained phenomena. Because you never know what's driven them to believe what they believe, but chances are, it's rooted in tragedy. Or anxiety. Or fear."

I thought about what had happened last night in the Haunted Village. I didn't want to admit it, even to myself, but for a moment I had understood what it could be like to believe. To hear something go bump in the night and fear that anything, even the impossible, seems possible. Real.

"There are good people, smart people, who believe in spirits. You would do yourself a favor to remember that, even when someone's beliefs seem silly to you."

I nodded. My tongue felt too big for my mouth. She squeezed my hand before pulling it away, a signal that I could go eat my cold toast at last.

* * *

I shouldn't have been surprised that Shaggy still hadn't responded to me by the time I reached my second planned destination: Burnett's jewelry store. But I admit I was a little hurt. I liked to think Shaggy and I had a special relationship, built on a shared preference for being left alone as much as possible.

Daphne was waiting for me outside. An overnight cold snap meant she was bundled up in a thick lavender parka, her red hair a curtain covering her face. When she saw me approach, her eyes lit up.

"Jinkies all recovered?"

I nodded and pointed to the door. "Shall we?"

Daphne whistled. "You're all business today, eh?"

"It's been a morning," I confided. "And now I just want to get this over with."

We had one mission with Noelle that morning: to ask her about the jewels that washed up and confirm that they were fake, and to convince her to tell the police as much. We'd considered showing her the ruby we'd found the night before, but we weren't sure if we wanted to tell anyone about it . . . not yet.

Burnett's was, as expected, completely empty except

for Noelle, who was sitting behind the register talking quietly on her phone. A new flyer was taped to the register: 25% OFF ALL ITEMS! When she saw us enter, she quickly hung up.

"Hi, girls." Her voice was cautious, guarded, but it turned hopeful at her next question. "Oh! Are you back for that beautiful bracelet? I saved it for you!"

Daphne's expression wavered before snapping back into its neutral, unreadable look. "Not yet, no."

"Well ..." Noelle's eyes lit up. "Are you here to pick Taylor up for the walk to school? I'm afraid you've just missed her."

We glanced at each other. "Um . . . no?" I said weakly.

"Oh," she said, her brow creasing. "That would've been . . . nice. Tell me, how's she been getting on?"

"Um ..." I stalled. Daphne covered for me in that casual, calm way she does.

"She's quiet, but I think she's warming up," she answered. It was the right thing to say—Noelle's expression cleared, and she nodded, seemingly content with that answer.

"I just really want her to fit in," Noelle said, almost apologetically.

We nodded while I thought about how embarrassed I'd be if my own mother ever said anything like that to other kids at school.

THE DARK DECEPTION

While we stood outside, Daphne and I had agreed to put the past behind us and pretend Noelle hadn't lied to our faces the other day. Daphne, true to form, pasted one of her trademark cheery smiles onto her face. (I, also true to form, did no such thing. My face was my face, and I was wholly unable to manipulate it to convey certain emotions the way Daphne could.)

"Cold enough for you this morning?" Daphne changed the subject and mimed a shiver.

"Sure is," Noelle agreed. "Aren't you going to be late for school?"

"On our way!" Daphne chirped.

Daphne's perkiness was giving me a headache. "We just stopped in to double-check something with you, since you're the expert and all," I put in.

Noelle raised her eyebrows questioningly, and I rushed ahead. "The jewels that washed up? What's your expert opinion on them?"

A twin set of creases formed in Noelle's forehead. "Expert opinion about what? I was here at the store the day they washed ashore, so I never saw them on the beach." She shrugged.

"Sure, but you're an expert," I pressed, stressing the final word.

"In jewelry? Yes," she said. "So?"

"So," I said, casting what I hoped wasn't a desperate

VELMA

look at Daphne, "you probably know about the density of rubies and emeralds and all that stuff."

Noelle sighed. "It's probably time for homeroom, so why don't you just get to the point?"

Ouch. "Fine. I will!" I said hotly.

Daphne jumped in. "What we're trying to establish is whether the density of real jewels makes them sink in water. Not float. And those jewels that washed up were definitely floating."

"Ah!" Noelle nodded. "Right. Emeralds and rubies and sapphires, all the stones that washed ashore the other day, should absolutely sink in water if they're real."

"Aha!" I slammed my hand down on the register. Daphne looked at me in surprise with just a tinge of alarm mixed in. "So in your expert opinion, those jewels can't be real! It's science."

"Not so fast." Noelle held up a hand. "Fresh water. Not salt."

I paused. "Come again?"

"Real stones sink in fresh water," Noelle explained. Her voice had taken on the overly patient tone of a kindergarten teacher. "But in salt water, the density changes. The water becomes heavier than the jewels. Many objects that sink in fresh water will float in salt water."

"I . . . um . . ." I was speechless. That couldn't be right. How could I have missed that simple, obvious fact? I stuffed my hands into my hoodie's pocket and touched the tissue covering the stone we'd found. In that moment, I was relieved we hadn't shown it to Noelle.

For the first time in my life, I hadn't done my homework correctly.

"Sorry to wreck whatever theory you were working on, but like I told the lieutenant, those jewels were real." She nodded twice for emphasis.

"You met with the police?" Daphne asked.

"Of course. They brought me in for help right away." Noelle smirked. "Like you said. I'm the expert."

DAPHNE

I DRAGGED A SHELL-SHOCKED Velma into school. By the time we reached our lockers, I had fully tuned her out. There were only so many ways I could hear my best friend beat herself up for forgetting one silly science fact.

Okay, maybe not silly. Honestly, I was a little peeved at Velma's mistake, and I was glad she was so busy blaming herself that I didn't have a chance to say a word. I wasn't mad because we had to scrap our theory and start all over again, but because I had almost staked my internship on it. I had almost told Milford Jones that the jewels were fake! I'd have been a laughingstock at the *Howler* once the truth came out. And that wasn't an easy feat to achieve, considering the *Howler*'s reputation for printing wild stories using the flimsiest of evidence.

Plus, my mind kept going back to what I'd seen in the Haunted Village the night before, and what we'd found. I wanted desperately to get the ruby appraised, but after what had just happened with Noelle, we'd have to find someone else to look at it. But I didn't know who to trust.

All this is to say, when I pulled Velma around the corner to get to our respective homerooms and we ran smack into Shaggy, neither of us were our best selves.

"Like, watch it!" Shaggy snapped. Great. He was in a mood, too. The three of us made quite a team.

Scratch that. *Four* of us. Because hiding behind Shaggy, practically invisible under his height, was Taylor Burnett.

"You're just the guy we wanted to see!" I searched deep within to find smooth, cool Daphne and smiled sweetly at Shaggy. I tried to hide my surprise at his more-rumpled-than-usual appearance. "Sorry for literally bumping into you, though."

"Everything okay, Shaggy?" Velma asked. She must have noticed the dark circles under his eyes, too. His baggy shirt had more wrinkles than everything in my entire basket of dirty laundry combined, and his hair was sticking up in every direction.

I won't lie: He was still pretty cute. Shaggy's vibe—carefree, loose—was so counter to my own ever-vigilant default state that it never failed to intrigue me on some cellular level. He was a curious creature, that Shaggy. No wonder I was so eager to figure out Marcy's warning about him.

I glanced at Taylor and smiled, trying to make up for snapping at her on the beach. "Hey. Taylor, right?"

She widened her eyes and nodded. I waited for her to say something—I don't know, maybe ask me my name like a normal person would?—but when she stayed mute, I shrugged it off and turned my attention back to Shaggy. "Here. I saw this and thought of you."

His eyes brightened just a little when he glimpsed the bag I extended his way, which gave away the surprise. Shaggy hadn't responded to Velma's offer of breakfast, but we'd picked up something for him anyway. Inside the bag was Crystal Cove's most famous breakfast sandwich: vegetarian bacon (aka facon), egg, cheese, and a pickle on a fresh-baked croissant.

"Whoa, thanks. This is my fave." He unwrapped it right there in the hallway, lockers slamming and kids laughing around us.

"Got a sec?" I asked. He shrugged. I took that as a yes. Most things I take as a yes. It's how I get what I want, most of the time.

I steered him to an empty, open classroom, hoping Taylor would get the picture and disappear. Instead, she followed us inside and awkwardly stood by the door as

Shaggy, Velma, and I sat at the first lab table. Velma immediately began fiddling with beakers someone had left there, while I stared meaningfully at her. She was supposed to lead the conversation, but apparently I was going to have to take this on while she brooded over every single science lesson she'd ever had, wondering how she'd gotten it wrong about the jewels.

"Shaggy," I began. My eyes darted over to Taylor, who was staring at the floor. Seriously, was this girl okay? I made a mental note to ask Shaggy later what her deal was. "Funny question for you! The other day, I think it was . . ."

I pretended to search my mind for the day, like I didn't already have it, plus the time and weather and the outfit I was wearing, indelibly stamped in my brain. (I have a very good memory, but it helps to disarm people sometimes.) Shaggy slurped a pickle that was threatening to fall out of his sandwich and just like that, my attraction to his overall demeanor lessened.

I snapped my fingers. "Saturday! Saturday morning. We were at The Mocha and saw you go into Burnett's jewelry store."

Shaggy kept eating, his eyes not moving from his croissant. Out of the corner of my eye, I saw Taylor's head flick up, her long hair forming a curtain over half her face. For a moment, in this light, her hair was less brown and more auburn. Red, even.

DAPHNE

Like the woman I'd seen in the Haunted Village.

I forced away the image (and the shiver down my spine that accompanied it) and forged ahead, the lie coming easily to me now. I would worry about what that said about me—that I could lie to someone I considered a friend so easily—later.

"We were in that store right before you, and I'm pretty sure I lost the new anklet I was wearing in there. It probably fell right off my ankle onto the carpet, ugh! Any chance you saw anything on the floor? Noelle couldn't find it, but I was hoping maybe Scooby did . . ."

Shaggy's head snapped up. "Sorry, Daph. But I, like, was surfing on Saturday morning. Like always."

That got Velma's attention, at least. She put down the beakers and turned her attention to Shaggy. "You're probably thinking of Sunday morning, Shag. But we saw you Saturday. You and Scooby headed right into Burnett's. Early."

Shaggy dropped the remaining scraps of his sandwich and stretched his long arms overhead, yawning. "Naw, man. Saturday, I surf. Sunday, I surf. Sometimes I even skip homeroom just so I can surf. It's, like, my favorite hobby."

"Shaggy," Velma tried again, "we saw you there. This past Saturday. Downtown."

He shrugged. "Like, sorry I can't tell you what you want to hear. But I wasn't at Burnett's on Saturday."

121

I drew in a deep breath, trying to figure out my next question. But before I could speak, Taylor cut in. "That's my mom's store."

I swiveled to face her. She'd spoken! Taylor was looking at me, all big eyes and earnest, and I felt a hot stone of annoyance sizzle deep within me.

"That's right," I said smoothly, like I had just made the connection, like this kid wasn't ruining my plan to get Shaggy to talk. "I met your mom the other day."

"I'd be happy to go there after school and look for your anklet," Taylor rushed on, the words spilling out of her mouth like she was desperate to spit them out. Desperate to make me happy. "Or I could even call my mom right now and have her look. What color was it? I can help!"

The bell rang, cutting her off.

I closed my eyes and tried to fight off the headache I could feel coming on. Shaggy was a wanderer. Ever since I'd known him, he'd spent hours on foot, Scooby trailing behind him, walking aimlessly around town. Was it possible he just didn't remember all the places he stopped in, or all the people he spoke to, on his many travels?

Or was he lying to us? Just like Noelle had. And if Noelle had lied to us once . . . who's to say she wouldn't hesitate to lie to us again? A sudden thought sparked inside me. Could we trust *any*thing Noelle said?

When I opened my eyes, they caught Velma's. She nodded once, almost imperceptibly. Obviously, Shaggy and Noelle had agreed to deny their Saturday morning visit. But why?

I glanced at Taylor. The color of her hair ... it really looked red in the bright morning light. Was she mixed up in all of this? Was she the one I'd seen last night? And was that why her mom was lying to me?

Shaggy didn't care about being late to homeroom, but Velma did, so I knew we were running out of time. "Sorry, my mistake. I must have my days wrong." I shrugged, projecting the same kind of attitude that he was: Like, wasn't everything so casual, weren't we all just so loose? But inside, a plan was clicking into place, all my levers and buttons shifting.

"Daphne's so bad at remembering things," Velma chimed in. Then she scowled. "Me too, apparently."

"Do you still need my help?" Taylor piped in, brushing her bangs out of her face. "Looking for the anklet?"

"Uh ... sure," I said, shrugging. I couldn't get a read on what was going on with Taylor. Was she trying to befriend us to dispel our suspicion? Or was she just a lonely teenager trying to make friends?

"I can also help you find anything else you're looking for. Like, at the store, I mean. Presents or something to wear for a special occasion ..."

I racked my brain. "Actually, my mother has a big

birthday coming up and I wanted to get her something special. A custom piece, maybe?"

That caught Shaggy's attention. "Like, yeah, Noelle can create something for your mom! She's awesome. The Burnetts have been customizing the Rogerses' family jewelry for, like, ever. There's a lotta history there, between the Rogerses and the Burnetts. We're the oldest family in Crystal Cove, and they're the second, you know."

Hmm, I thought while Taylor nodded enthusiastically.

"By the way," Shaggy said, shooting up from his seat with more energy than he typically exerted. "Party tonight. You're coming, right?"

Velma pursed her lips, but I smiled at Shaggy. "Obviously."

* * *

By lunchtime the *Howler* had plastered their latest headline all over social media: *Connection between Washed-Up Jewels and Reports of Unusual Activities? Cops Launch Official Investigation.*

By the time the final bell rang, my nerves were shot. Not from the horrible trigonometry test I'd forgotten about, but from the stupid pranksters who'd thought it would be clever to hide behind open doors and lockers and yell "Boo!" at anyone they could find. Rumors of ghosts were on everyone's lips; it felt like no one in school could talk about anything else. Even the Hex Girls, normally so intimidating as they stomped around the halls, seemed subdued, whispering to each other in the cafeteria and glaring at anyone who dared venture near them. Of course, I guess once you've been kidnapped and trapped in an underground sea cave the way Thorn, Luna, and Dusk had been—the work of Dr. Hunter and my own aunt Emma— you take any threat a little more seriously, even this one.

I was very ready to leave school and escape to the soothing sounds of keyboards tapping and phones ringing at the *Howler*.

But Milford must've felt the same raw edginess I felt— like another shoe was about to drop, and this time it wouldn't be something like jewels washing up. It would be ugly. And he needed to be ready. Or rather, *we*, the *Howler* staff, needed to be ready to hear him say it.

When I arrived, Milford was standing on a chair outside his office, arms flailing, as the entire *Howler* team looked at their shoes, their computers, the sunny day outside— anywhere but at the man who was screaming at them.

"Do you see this?" Milford was saying as I stepped off the elevators and into the chaos. He waved his phone around. I walked noiselessly to my desk, trying to be as unobtrusive as possible. Did he expect people to be able to read his tiny screen from their seats? I wondered.

Apparently not, because then he read, word for word, the story on his screen.

THE DARK DECEPTION

"From the *San Francisco Bay Post*," he boomed. "Headline: 'More Scares Than Answers in the Tiny Town of Crystal Cove.' Lede: 'Crystal Cove, California, famous for its video game of the same name but infamous for its residents' peculiar insistence on believing in the supernatural'"—Milford paused for effect, peering over his phone at us before finishing—"'is reckoning with a new threat: whether the half a million dollars' worth of jewels that washed up on its shores over the weekend is a sign of the supernatural, or simply something more feasible, such as' yadda, yadda, yadda."

Milford pocketed his phone and pointed at his team. I noticed Ram leaning against the doorframe to Milford's office, as though he'd been in there when Milford decided ranting to his entire staff was a solid idea. He really had earned Milford's respect, I realized.

"Compare that to our boring headline from this morning," Milford said. Then he rubbed his forehead as though he had a headache—I could relate—and softened his voice. "Folks. FOLKS. Your job, *our* job, is to be the single source of information about Crystal Cove to the rest of the world, and to keep the people coming back to *us*. To do that, we need intrigue. We need mystery. We need compelling stories that inform people of every possibility!"

My brow furrowed. I'd always known Milford was all about page clicks, but he was dangerously close to saying

DAPHNE

outright that his paper's goal was readership, not, you know, *news*. For a moment, I allowed myself to think about what would happen if I told him and Ram about what Velma and I had seen the night before. But no. I'd promised Velma we'd keep the ruby a secret till we could figure out who to ask about it. The last thing she'd want was Milford plastering our latest clue all over the Howler before we had a chance to investigate.

Milford finished his monologue with what I assumed he thought was a rousing speech about the importance of journalism, but was really a passive-aggressive way of telling the reporters to do better, and disappeared back into his office. Within minutes, the *Howler* floor was back to normal—printers printing, keyboards clacking, coffee machine brewing.

Out of the corner of my eye I watched Ram circle around the room, nodding hello and slapping high fives in that way guys do to other guys. I've been called popular my whole life, but mine has always been a removed popularity, a distant one. People think they know me and my story, but they only know what I let them know. Watching Ram made me realize how different his popularity was. He was open. Authentic. I didn't know Ram much (yet), but already I felt like I was closer to him than some of the "friends" I'd known for years.

It made me wonder if there was another way for me, too.

I busied myself checking my emails so that Ram wouldn't

think I was staring at him when he dropped into his seat.

"Hey, Blake," he said warmly. I whirled around to smile at him. *Poof.* There went my pretense at being busy. "How was school?"

Ugh. I'd convinced myself that Ram hadn't heard Velma's announcement of my age the other day. I mumbled something about it being fine and quickly changed the subject. "Seems like you-know-who is in a mood."

"Yeah, he's definitely got some BEE today," Ram laughed. At my expression, he explained, "Big Editor Energy. But he liked my story, so."

"What's your story?" I asked eagerly.

He clicked over to the *Howler*'s home page and swiveled his screen around to show me. There, in a massive font size, was a headline that made me wince: *Washed-Up Jewels Continue to Shock Crystal Cove as All Signs Point to the Vanished Returning.*

"That's . . . uh . . ." I searched for the words. Even in the few seconds that I watched, the Share count on the story doubled. I felt a swirl of nausea in my stomach, knowing that right this very moment, hundreds of people were reading this headline and having their worst fears confirmed—that the jewels *were* supernatural in origin, that they *did* have to be afraid of ghosts. The fact that the *Howler* was giving legitimacy to these outrageous, unproven claims was . . . irresponsible, at best. Immoral at worst.

DAPHNE

I drummed my fingers on my desk to stall for time. I didn't want Ram to think I was judging his story. Then again, I was totally judging his story.

"It's a lot, I know," Ram said easily, like he knew what I was about to say but didn't take it too seriously. "I've definitely learned to pivot my writing style at this place. Milford likes a provocative thesis. But on the upside, I'm pretty sure I'll win this competition my friends at school and I have going."

"What's the competition?"

"It's kind of a tradition in my department. At the end of each semester, we tally up page views of all the stories we've published. The student with the most wins this stupid trophy that gets passed around." He shrugged. "Bragging rights, mostly."

"Oh," I said, considering this. "Cool . . . ?"

"Don't say that on my account, Blake. It's not cool, it's dumb. But . . . I don't know. I'm just playing the game, I guess."

See? That's what I meant about Ram being so much more authentic than I could ever imagine being. Because I was playing a game, too, wasn't I? The clothes, my makeup, everything . . . I'd created this Daphne Blake persona because I knew she would win everyone over, and I could get what I wanted that way. I could manipulate people by smiling, or by ignoring. Ram was at least brave enough to

129

THE DARK DECEPTION

openly admit he was playing, but I could never stomach anyone knowing how nakedly ambitious I was.

"Anyway." I switched gears and pointed to his screen. "That headline is certainly a choice. It's probably not what anyone at Crystal Cove High needs to see after the day we've had."

I filled him in on school—the rumors, the caution, the pranks. How I watched some freshman dissolve in tears after telling her friends that she'd called the police that morning to report a mysterious prowler in her family's yard, and how two sophomores got into an actual fistfight after disagreeing about whether Crystal Cove was haunted or not. "People are really on edge."

Ram sighed, leaning back in his chair. He stretched his arms up and I tried to avert my eyes from the lean, muscle-y swath of stomach that showed as his button-down shirt lifted an inch. But when he placed his hands over his eyes and sighed, remaining still (and clearly conflicted) for a few moments, I forgot about his body. "Hey. You okay?"

"Ugh," he sputtered, rubbing at his face. When his eyes met mine, they were bloodshot. Ram looked tired. "You're right, Blake. I got carried away with winning. I probably shouldn't be encouraging Milford with these kinds of stories."

"I mean, the story's the story, right?" I treaded carefully, keeping my voice light and my attention on my own screen.

DAPHNE

"If there are actual ghosts here, let the facts speak for themselves."

My tone was casual, but I held my breath at Ram's response. He was a college student. He'd taken way more journalism classes and workshops than I had. (I'd taken exactly zero, so that wasn't hard to achieve. But still.) This was his second year interning at the *Howler*. I didn't want him to think I was some hotshot kid trying to tell him what to do. I didn't want him thinking I was a kid at all!

Ram stared at his screen, at his own headline, for a while. I busied myself, clicking around randomly and pretending to type an email. Finally, he straightened up and began pounding at his keyboard.

"I'm submitting a correction request to the digital team right now," he announced. I hid a smile of relief while a burst of something that felt a lot like pride overrode my earlier nausea. I was glad—thrilled, actually—to see Ram changing course and doing the right thing here.

"What about Milford?"

"I can handle Milford," Ram said. He paused. "Well. I think. He's definitely going to be mad, but I think I can find a way to spin it. I know what makes him tick."

The thought of asking—no, telling—Milford that a story title that was racking up shares and clicks needed to be revised—rewritten to be made less compelling, less scary—after the speech he'd just delivered would have

131

made me curl up into a ball and hide under my desk. But I could tell Ram was nervous about the idea, and I wanted to support him in making this good but challenging decision, so I made him an offer. "Do you want me to come with you?"

"No way!" He pointed at me. "You're awesome, Blake, but this is my fault and my responsibility to fix."

I grinned. I was glad he saw it that way, too, and I'd barely had to lift a finger to get him to change his mind. To see the error of his ways. This is what I mean when I say my power has always been in making people do what I want, but getting them to think it's their idea.

And right now, I didn't even feel guilty about it.

It's always like this on nights she performs: a slickening of the hands, a loosening of the throat. Her whole body changes when she begins to assemble the instruments, to walk the stage. She paints on a dark lipstick and instantly she is transformed.

There is something else tonight, too, though; a different kind of transformation. She can feel it in the air. She adjusts the mic stand, pulling it up until it reaches her mouth, and looks out onto the empty lawn. Soon enough, it will be crowded with people. They will gaze at her and move at her command, and that is a unique kind of magic no one can bottle. And it belongs to her.

Onstage, she is anyone. Everyone. An energy shoots out of her and mingles with the crowd, becoming something new, something one of a kind. She sings for all of them; none of them. She sings for herself; for someone else. She sings for acceptance, for expression, for the possibilities that lie ahead. Maybe, most of all, she sings for love.

For her.

She blushes, grateful the party hasn't started yet and no one is here to see her fall to pieces. She tests the mic—"One two, one two"—and adjusts some knobs, furiously fighting the flood of emotions that rise up her throat at the thought of that one person.

She doesn't expect a response from her mic test, so when her own voice echoes back to her—"One two, one two"— her heart leaps. She scans the backyard. The pool bubbles with turquoise water; the deck is strung with sparkling white lights. The sun is setting and long shadows stretch across the grass, climbing over the stage, clawing at her feet. She studies them with interest, lifting up one foot and then another, testing to see if the shadows will follow her.

Hush.

What was that? She's alone onstage and, she thought, alone in the yard. The rest of the band is still painting on their stage makeup, warming up their vocals. The party will start soon.

"Hello?" she says into the mic. Her voice, throaty and full, booms over the speakers.

It's just nerves, she tells herself. She knows she will probably be here tonight: The one she sings to. The one she sings for.

But what if she doesn't appreciate the singing? What if the singing, and the persona that goes with it, is the very thing blocking them from being together?

The sun is fully set now, bathing the yard in amber light.

Click.

The spotlight she had positioned behind the pool earlier suddenly turns on, blinding her. "Hey!" she cries, shading her eyes. Her heart begins to thump. "Who did that?"

No one answers. She blinks until her eyes adjust. She peers into the yard, searching the shadows. But no one is there.

A tingle grows on her palms, soon spreading over her wrists and up her arms. She's never had stage fright before and wonders, briefly, if this is what it feels like. Is she caus-ing her own freak-out? Is she making her feel like the night is off-kilter, like the air around her is about to burst into flames? Should she even sing at all? Maybe she should get off the stage, take off the lipstick. Be herself, plain and simple, and ask her out for coffee.

The pool catches her eye. The bubbles are multiplying. Steam is pooling in the corners, thickening and rising.

Click.

The light disappears. Someone has turned off the spotlight.

She is scared now, and she can't even articulate why. "Hello?" *she tries again, into the mic.* "Who's there?"

The mist over the pool rises, crawls over the cement and the deck chairs. It spreads over the lawn, gray and thick

She's voiceless suddenly. She tries to clear her throat, to say something. She tries to sing. But she is frozen, helpless, as the mist encircles the stage. Something that feels like fear, like horror, grips her insides.

"Sing," *a voice from the mist demands.*

Her throat unlocks. "Help," *she whispers. The mic catches it, loops it, so now it's playing on repeat throughout the lawn: help, help, help, help.*

She opens her mouth, tests a note. The mic captures it. She has an image of her voice being snatched, locked away in a drawer.

THE DARK DECEPTION

Is it her imagination, or does the mist retreat a little at the sound of her voice?

She tries again. Full and low, she sings. There; she can see a little better now. The fog is dissipating. Thinning.

Her heart hollows.

It's a sign. She knows this now.

Sing for them. Sing for her.

Sing, or else.

VELMA

IT'S NOT THAT I'VE never been wrong before. I'm sure, at some point in my life—maybe even many points!—I've gotten things mixed up. I've probably gotten an answer or two incorrect on a quiz, for example. And I do remember a day in second grade when a snowstorm was predicted to hit us; I'd persuaded Daphne to skip her book report, since I was positive school would be canceled. It turned out to be just a rainstorm, though, and poor Daphne had to write her report on the bus.

But other than that, I had a pretty good track record of being right. Which was why I couldn't seem to get over the stupid, stupid mistake I'd made.

"Literally, when will you stop talking about this?" Daphne's voice, coming from her bedroom, was high on

THE DARK DECEPTION

the exasperation scale. I didn't blame her. But I was more exasperated than she was.

I answered from her bathroom, where I was staring at myself in the mirror. "Literally? Probably never."

Out of habit, I went to push up my glasses, but ended up jabbing myself on the bridge of my nose. It was Tuesday afternoon. My contacts had arrived, and I'd spent the afternoon figuring out how to put them in. My first few attempts had been such a disaster that I'd ended up at Daphne's house, where her vanity, lined with Hollywood-grade lighting, had helped. Now I couldn't stop looking at my reflection. Without my trademark glasses, I looked, somehow, both older and younger at the same time.

"Whoa," Daphne said as I stepped out of her bathroom and blinked in the bright light.

"This feels weird." I patted around my eyes. "Do I . . . you know."

"What?"

I shuffled my feet for a few seconds, feeling my face grow hot. "Do I look funny?"

"Velma." Daphne got up from her bed, where she'd been lounging and playing with her phone—probably scouring Ram's social media feeds, not that she'd ever admit it—and grabbed my shoulders, peering at my face. "I've said it before, and I'll say it again. You're hot. Whether you're wearing glasses or not, you're hot. Now can we go to this party already?"

"Why, again?" I muttered. I wasn't in the mood for a party. (Honestly, was I ever?) But tonight in particular felt heavy, weighted with not just my stupid mistake but with all the ghosts who were waiting for us to prove they weren't real.

I needed to find out why someone would dump jewels— especially jewels worth a significant amount of money—into the ocean. Not to mention prowling around the Haunted Village with them. Because once I figured out the *why*, I could narrow down the *who*.

"How many reasons should I list?" Daphne began counting off on her fingers. "So we can see Shaggy and figure out why he's lying to us. Because it's a weeknight and there's nothing else to do. Or maybe so you can debut your new look. Or, I know! So we can, for just one minute, stop talking about ghosts and jewels and the Vanished, and do something normal for once?"

"Since when does going to one of Shaggy's parties count as normal?"

Daphne fixed me with a glare. "I know you hate to admit it, but parties can actually be fun. Most teenagers think so! Besides, the last time you went—"

"First time," I interrupted.

"You were on a mission to yell at Marcy, and you and I weren't . . . well, you know. Speaking."

Oh, I remembered.

"So this one will be different," Daphne concluded.

"Where'd his parents go, anyway?" I flashed back to the look on Mr. Rogers's face at the beach the day the jewels washed ashore. He was definitely a guy who seemed like he needed a vacation.

Daphne shrugged. "Who knows? That guy always has somewhere exotic to be. Or maybe he wanted to protect Shaggy's mom from the ghosts of Crystal Cove." She made a silly face, as if to say the idea was preposterous, but I knew Daphne well enough to know that part of her was probably wishing she'd made the same plans. It wasn't that Daphne believed in ghosts, necessarily; it was more that she didn't *not* believe.

We finished getting ready, which for me meant retying the laces on my combat boots and making sure my phone was charged, and for Daphne meant changing out of the dress and blazer she'd worn to the *Howler* offices and back into jeans. She pulled on some kind of complicated top that had ties dangling all over it, which she knotted with ease. Then she added lipstick and swapped out her diamond studs for a pair of long earrings that looked like half-moons, brushed her hair until it shone, and grabbed her purse.

"Ready?"

I bit my tongue.

VELMA

When we finally made it to Shaggy's house, my eyes were watering from the cold.

"Stop touching your eyes." Daphne swatted my hand.

"This feels too weird!" I complained. The wind whipped through Shaggy's front yard.

"You're too weird. No one's even going to notice you're wearing contacts, they'll just think you got a haircut or something. People don't really pay attention to other people."

I shivered under my black jacket and stared at the Rogers estate as Daphne trotted up the front stairs to the oversized entrance. It was hard not to; the house was so big, it was nearly impossible for my eyes to avoid it no matter where they landed. She rang the bell and then, seeing that I wasn't next to her like she'd thought, huffed, stomped back down the stairs, grabbed me by the elbow, and pulled me up.

Aimee Drake opened the double doors. "Daphne!"

Daphne's smile was bright and, I noticed straightaway, a level six on the fake scale. That meant Aimee was tolerable but just barely.

"So glad you made it. You've been totally MIA lately, you know that?" Aimee trilled. She shot me a glance and then whispered something in Daphne's ear.

"What was that?" I said loudly. Aimee blushed and disappeared into the crowd while Daphne chuckled into her hand.

And what a crowd it was. The entrance to the house was

THE DARK DECEPTION

grand and imposing, flanked by two matching grand staircases and centered by a glittering chandelier. It shed sparkles over the crowd, who were eating—Shaggy's parties always had tons of food—and dancing. I was too short to see over the countless heads around me, but I knew the great room, where I'd spent countless sleepovers, was just to the left of the entrance, and the formal living room was to the right. I was sure those spaces were crammed with people, too.

"I need some air," I mumbled. I started for the backyard, which I knew was through the long hallway where old-fashioned portraits of various Rogerses lived, their eyes following me until I reached the sliding doors that led to the back deck. Daphne hadn't told me she was following me, but I knew she was by the way the crowd parted for us—well, for her—as well as by the many greetings and smiles thrown my way. *Her* way.

"I wonder where Shaggy is," Daphne said as we surveyed the backyard. The deck was two stories, a far cry from the rickety old patio that had been here when we were kids. We followed the music to the edge and looked at the pool, which was heated (a few kids were splashing around) and underlit by spotlights, so that bright pinks and greens lapped the water. Daphne gasped. "Whoa."

I nodded, speechless. "I didn't realize I was missing all this by not coming to these parties."

"Believe me, you're not. He's never done this before!"

VELMA

"This" was a stage set up at the far end of the pool, outfitted with professional lighting and sound, including strobe lights pulsing to the sound of the beat. Onstage, the Hex Girls were in the throes of one of their wildest songs, and the crowd was rapt. I stared, entranced, my eyes skipping over Luna, pounding the keyboards while swaying her hips, and Dusk, hitting the drums and baring her fangs. Thorn was thrashing at her guitar and pouring out her heart into the microphone. I couldn't tear my eyes away.

"Earth to Velma." Daphne nudged me and pointed. "Target acquired."

Shaggy was hanging out by a long table piled high with food, with what looked like a sandwich in one hand and a candy bar in the other. He was talking earnestly to someone I'd never seen before; he had to be in his twenties, and he had to be related to Shaggy—that sandy hair and broad forehead were an unmistakable genetic gift from the Rogers family. Next to them was Taylor, doing what Taylor was quickly becoming known for: standing still, quietly surveying the crowd. I frowned. Why did it always seem like she was watching and waiting? I was starting to understand why Daphne was suspicious of her.

It took us a while to make our way over to Shaggy. I kept catching flashes of girls' earrings and necklaces and rings as they shone in the moving spotlights; every one of them hammered home my mission: We had to figure out the story behind those jewels. Only then would the rumors about ghosts finally end.

I crossed my fingers as Daphne pushed our way through the makeshift dance floor next to the pool. The truth is, though, I didn't think Crystal Cove would ever fully surrender its hold on the supernatural. And what did that say about those of us who lived here?

"You're a hard guy to find," Daphne said, by way of greeting, once we'd finally reached Shaggy. The Hex Girls were taking a break, and the ripple of silence in their wake made me realize how serious I suddenly felt. I swallowed my nerves and tried to channel Daphne's calm, cool vibe.

"Like, what? Velma Dinkley?" Shaggy nearly fell over at my presence. "Two parties in a row? What did I do to deserve this?"

"This is quite the shindig," I replied. I nodded at Taylor and then stuck my hand out to Shaggy's friend/relative. "I'm Velma."

He shook it, his face crinkling into a smile. "Jack Rogers."

"This is, like, my favorite cousin! Daphne, Velma, meet Jack." Shaggy looked proudly at his cousin. "I basically threw this party in his honor."

"Oh man," Jack groaned. "Don't tell me that, bro."

I furrowed my brow. My understanding was that Shaggy's parties were secret; how was he going to keep this one from his dad?

VELMA

"How long are you visiting for?" Daphne asked.

"A couple of weeks. I help Shaggy's dad out with the family businesses and had some meetings to take in person." Jack had a little bit of sandy-colored scruff on his chin; he scratched it absentmindedly. Something about his posture gave me pause; while he looked like Shaggy, he didn't move like him. He was stiff and uneasy; the opposite of Shaggy's visible comfort.

Shaggy whistled. Within seconds, Scooby came bounding through the crowd, landing at Shaggy's heels. As I scratched Scooby's ears, Shaggy said to his cousin, "I don't know how anyone can handle working with my dad, but you make it look easy."

"Me?" Jack scoffed. "No way, dude. I just have to work with the guy. You have to *live* with him. He's my uncle and I love him, but . . . man . . ."

I waited for Jack to finish his thought, eager to hear someone else's opinion about Shaggy's dad, but instead he crammed the remains of a bag of chips into his mouth and wiped the crumbs from his shirt—proof that their foreheads and coloring were definitely not the only genetic traits Shaggy and Jack shared.

"I haven't seen you around Crystal Cove before," I offered. My mind was whirring and clicking, trying to sort out Jack and his place in the Rogers family. I had a hunch he fit in, somehow, with the secret Shaggy was keeping; with the help Marcy said he needed. But seeing Jack here at one of Shaggy's famous parties felt off somehow—he was a Shaggy lookalike without the dog, without the surfer lingo. Like he was Shaggy from another dimension, one where he'd ditched the beach in favor of the boardroom.

"I don't visit too much," Jack said, scanning the crowd. I had a sickening thought.

"When did you arrive in town?"

"Jeez, Velma, take it down a notch," Daphne instructed under her breath. I elbowed her four times, which I hoped she would decipher to mean *I have a plan.*

"Um . . ." Jack scratched his chin. He looked to Shaggy for help. "Saturday?"

"Friday," Shaggy confirmed. "I remember because, like, it was raining, right? And your flight was way delayed? And I ended up eating all the pizza I'd ordered for you by myself?"

Hmm. Theoretically, a Friday arrival meant Jack would have had plenty of time to scatter the jewels into the ocean before Saturday morning. Why, I wasn't sure. But still, it was a lead worth exploring. I made a mental note to check Friday's flight delays to see if his story held up.

"I'm new in town, too," Taylor suddenly said, giving us a little wave, as though we hadn't already greeted her. *She's definitely weird*, I thought, and then immediately felt bad about thinking it. I knew what it was like to be branded the outsider, the strange one. But wow, Taylor was wasn't doing herself any favors.

"Right," I deadpanned.

Daphne gave me a look. "Where are you from again?" she asked Taylor.

Taylor's eyes lit up. It was the most animated I'd ever seen her. "Arizona. My parents, um, well, my mom, she wanted to come back home."

"Mmm," Daphne said, surveying the crowd. Taylor was losing her, and she seemed to sense it, so she rushed in to fill the silence.

"It's good for my mom to be back, but it definitely sucks moving in the middle of the school year," Taylor spilled. I raised my eyebrows. "But hey, at least now we have a chance to help right some wrongs here."

I frowned. Before I could ask her what she meant by that, Shaggy's face changed. "Fred! Dude!"

I froze, wondering why I was having trouble breathing. Fred Jones, tall and movie-star handsome, burst into our circle, bringing with him that easy energy that made everyone think they were his one and only best friend; the kind that made every straight girl think they were destined to be his true love. I reached for my glasses before remembering they were no longer there, and as a result, my hand hung, awkwardly, midair.

Shaggy introduced Jack to Fred while I tried to move

my arm out of the way and pretend I'd meant to do it all along. "Why are you moving like a robot?" Daphne hissed into my ear. Casual Velma, that's me!

I felt the unmistakable heat of someone's eyes boring into my face. Slowly, I looked up. It was Fred. Fred Jones was staring at me, his face questioning but also something else, something I couldn't quite decipher.

Fred was my childhood friend, the kid who was game for anything, back when we ran Mystery Inc. These days, Fred was Mr. Congeniality; everyone's favorite date to the dance. Tall and limber, he was always pulling some wild physical stunt to catch people's attention—or maybe divert it, I wasn't sure which.

"What?" I barked at him. I heard Daphne sigh, but I couldn't find the courage to meet her eyes.

Fred considered my question, cocking his head and studying my face. My nerves bubbled over into a chuckle that burst from my chest. Daphne closed her eyes for a moment, like she couldn't bear to watch.

"Velma." Fred said my name like it was a statement.

I wiggled my eyebrows at him. "Yes, Fred, Velma Dinkley. I promise we've met before."

Daphne let out a low moan while Fred's eyes took on a twinkle. "Aha. It's the glasses."

I felt heat shoot up from my lungs and pool in my cheeks as Fred stared at me. His staring made Shaggy stare, too, which made Jack stare. Thankfully, Daphne, sensing my discomfort, clapped her hands once. Four heads turned from me to her, and just like that, natural order was restored. "Shaggy, you got a minute?"

Panic—or something awfully close to it—flashed across Shaggy's face before it resettled into its usual laid-back expression. "Like, always. I just have to . . ."

Shaggy mumbled something and then, taking a page from the Vanished, he disappeared, swallowed by the crowd. Jack too.

Daphne and I gaped at each other.

"So," Fred said, like he was having his own separate conversation in his head that he'd suddenly decided to share with the rest of us, "what made you ditch the glasses? They were your . . . you know. Thing."

My thing. *My thing?* I'd hoped my "thing" would be a little more substantive than just the lenses I wore so I could see the world around me. But it was good, I realized, helpful even, to know that's how Fred Jones saw me. I was just a girl with big glasses.

"Hey, Fred, how's Jacqui Parker doing?" Daphne asked pointedly. Fred tore his eyes from mine and gave Daphne a questioning glance.

"Uh. Fine? How would I know?"

"Last I heard you were dating her," Daphne said through gritted teeth.

"Oh, no," he said quickly. Too quickly, I thought. He stared at me so intently I wondered if he was doing some kind of measurement of my face. "No, I'm single."

"For once." Daphne's big smile belied her snark. I could tell Fred wasn't sure of whether she was making fun of him or not. I tapped my foot—the Hex Girls had just come back onstage, and Dusk was tapping at the drums—and tried to escape the intensity of Fred's gaze. I did the only thing I could think of: I changed the subject.

"Fred, have you ever met Jack before?"

"Who? Oh, Shaggy's cousin or whatever? Never heard of him." He shook his head. Well, that was weird. Shaggy and Fred were pretty good friends. You'd think Shaggy would have mentioned him.

"Velma." Fred said my name again, and again it felt like a statement. Exasperated, I glared at him.

"What?"

"Wanna dance?"

I blinked. He held out a hand. I blinked again. Fred Jones . . . asking me to dance? With him? This had to be a joke of some kind. One of Fred's classic pranks.

As if he read my mind, he added, "Seriously. I love this song."

The Hex Girls were playing a cover of a slow, intimate song from one of my favorite singers. Which meant that Fred and I liked the same music. I didn't know why,

150

but I found that shocking. Maybe Fred wasn't who I thought he was.

I accepted his hand and he pulled me onto the dance floor. I tried to ignore the curious glances we received, but honestly, I didn't blame them. No one was more surprised at this dance than I was.

Fred wrapped his arms around my waist and I rested mine against his neck as we swayed. We didn't say a word, and I wondered what he was thinking.

Before the song ended, he let me know. "I seriously can't get over you without your glasses."

"Try," I suggested.

"It's just . . . wow. You look so different. Why'd you do it?"

"Why did I get contacts?" I tried not to let my annoyance bleed into my tone, but I was definitely feeling peeved. "So I can see, I guess. And because my new glasses kept falling off my face."

Fred, uncharacteristically, began to trip over his words. "Well, you look great. I mean, they look great. I mean, your face without contacts . . ."

"Looks great," I finished for him. I swallowed the lump that was forming in my throat. I couldn't even explain why I suddenly needed to cry, other than to say that I had wanted Fred to notice *me*. All of me. Not just my face.

THE DARK DECEPTION

When the song ended and the Hex Girls transitioned into something louder and faster, I released my arms and stepped away from Fred, too mortified to meet his eyes. He called my name, but I pretended not to hear it over Thorn's high note.

DAPHNE

AS SOON AS VELMA danced off with Fred, Nisha and Shawna accosted me.

"Girrrrrrl! This party, though!" Nisha said, air-kissing me.

"We never see you anymore," Shawna pouted. "Now that you have that 'important' job."

I ignored the way Shawna used air quotes around the word *important* and plastered on a smile. "Yeah, my internship is keeping me pretty busy." I left out the more important truth, which was that, even if I hadn't scored the internship, I'd have found some way to limit my time with Shawna. She and Nisha—and, come to think of it, a lot of my so-called friends—were part of my social circle mostly by default. We hung out together because we were all popular; we were all popular because we hung out together. It was a real chicken-or-the-egg situation.

I distracted myself by picturing Nisha and Shawna dressed up as chickens so as not to get annoyed at the way they were making fun of Velma as she danced with Fred.

"Oh. My. God. Are my eyes deceiving me?" Nisha mock-gasped.

"Did Detective Dinkley get contacts? Oh, that is too much!" Shawna giggled.

"All the better to see ghosts with," Nisha cracked.

"Ugh, don't say the G-word," Shawna cried. "*Something* creepy is happening here, and I don't like it."

"Speaking of creepy, have you seen that new kid?" Nisha rolled her eyes.

"How could I not? The girl is constantly staring at everybody!" Shawna mimicked what could only be Taylor Burnett by pulling her bangs over her wide eyes, ducking down to appear shorter, and making a goofy face at Nisha, who cracked up.

"Daph, please tell me you've noticed her," Nisha said through giggles. "What a freak!"

I mean, *freak* was a little harsh, but Shawna's impression did make me smile. As usual, though, Shawna took it a step further than necessary by adding, "She's so obsessed with Shaggy. Can you imagine them hooking up? She'd need a stepladder, she's so tiny!"

I rolled my eyes. They landed on Taylor, who was—no surprise—standing nearby, watching us.

And she'd surely overheard every word.

"Wait," I called out weakly as she flushed, ducked her head, and ran away, practically diving under bodies to escape.

"Well, she needed to hear it," Nisha said, shrugging.

"Rude," I muttered, grabbing my phone at the first hint of a vibration. They were *so* not worth the fight. I checked my text alert and then double-checked it, certain I was hallucinating.

It was Ram. **Daphne, just wanted to thank you again for your advice today. You were right! You free tomorrow for a coffee?**

"Hey."

I'd gotten so lost in reading—and rereading—Ram's words that I hadn't realized Velma was back, or that the song had changed. Or even, I realized, glancing around, that Nisha and Shawna—and Taylor, of course—were gone. Good riddance.

Velma looked much less dreamy than I'd anticipated she'd look after her first dance, her first anything, with Fred, whom I knew for a fact she had a crush on. Then again, half of my brain was still absorbing that text message, wondering whether Ram was asking me for a coffee, or a coffee *date*. The difference was significant.

"How was that?" I wiggled my eyebrows. Velma's face fell.

"I told you I didn't want to come to this stupid party," she grumbled. Uh-oh. I struggled to find something to say in response. Finally, I just reverted to what I hoped was a safe subject: the jewels.

"Why don't we do what we came here for," I suggested, "and find Shaggy. Get him to answer our questions. For real this time."

"He's just going to dodge us again. Or lie to us." She shook her head, avoiding my eyes. "Guys suck."

"Okay . . ." I pocketed my phone. I knew at least one guy who didn't suck—yet—and he'd just texted me for a date. Or something. Maybe it was Ram's age that made him so cool, so mature, so real, I thought. College guys were different. Right?

I jumped out of the way when two sophomores nearly crashed into me as they threw a football around. Yes, college guys had to be different. I was sure of it. "Let's go."

While the noise level in the house was more manageable, the volume of people was somehow even higher, and I lost Velma somewhere between the kitchen and the study. Good, I thought. I wanted to give her a minute to cool down from whatever happened with Fred.

Everyone knew the only rule Shaggy had about his parties was to stay downstairs. Luckily, not everyone knew about the secret back staircase, the one we used to hide in every time Shaggy hosted a sleepover. It was tucked back in a far corner of the kitchen. I made my way over and, when I was pretty sure no one was looking, darted up them.

Ah, quiet. Or at least, not the pounding bass that had overtaken the first floor. Just in case, I skipped over the fifth stair—it used to be super creaky, and I didn't want to take the risk—and padded down the upstairs hallway.

The second floor was mostly dark and mostly quiet, but at the end of the hallway I noticed some light peeking out from under a door. As I crept closer, I remembered what the room was: Mr. Rogers's study. Shaggy used to call it his war room, the place where he kept a bunch of random family heirlooms—photo albums and chipped plates and vases, but also military artifacts from various Rogers family members' service, like old uniforms and helmets. Weird, but I guess every family had its skeletons. Some more so than others, I thought as I walked past yet another creepy portrait.

I crept closer. My heart thrummed loudly inside my chest. I could hear my own pulse inside my ears; it drowned out the music downstairs, the sound of my footsteps.

Another step; then another. The door to the war room was fast approaching. What was my game plan? I wondered. Was I going to burst in and yell "Gotcha!"—or was I going to stay outside the door and eavesdrop? I had to decide. Time was running out.

And then someone decided for me.

* * *

A hand grasped my shoulder. I yelped.

The hand covered my mouth. Gasping for breath, I fumbled to lift my elbow and hit the ghost in the—

"Velma?" I wheezed, doubled over, catching my breath.

"Shh!" she hushed. She pulled us back into an open door—one of the several guest bathrooms that lined this floor—and then ducked out her head, peeking up and down the hallway. "Coast is clear."

"What are you doing? You scared me to death!" My heart was beating double time now, frantic, like it was desperate to escape my body.

She had the decency to look ashamed. "Sorry. But I figured you'd be up here looking for Shaggy, and then I saw you getting closer to the war room, and I thought I'd save you from yourself."

I rubbed my shoulder where she'd grabbed me. "What's that supposed to mean?"

Velma shot me a look. "Come on. You were totally going to kick open the door and yell 'aha!'"

"I—" I paused. She kinda had me there.

Velma nodded, smirking. "I just think we need a better plan," she explained. She looked at the floor. "I need

DAPHNE

tonight to not be a total bust. We need answers—either about the jewels, or about Shaggy. Preferably both."

I studied Velma for a few beats. For a girl who'd just danced with the guy she was crushing on, she seemed way down. "What's up, V?"

She sighed and played with the zipper on her jacket. "I overheard Aimee Drake telling Aparna Din that Fred only asked me to dance because . . . because . . ."

I scowled. "Because of your new contacts?"

"What?" She snapped up her head. "I wish. No. They said that Shaggy had asked Fred to keep me occupied. To keep me away from him because I was, and I quote, 'going all Detective Dinkley on him.'"

I dropped my head into my hands and groaned. "Oh, V. I am so sorry that dumb nickname keeps coming back up. It's not even a funny insult! I don't know why they keep saying it!"

Velma held up a hand. "It's fine. Honestly. I barely even care about the nickname. I just . . ."

I nodded, but I was burning inside, my throat swelling. I'd made up Velma's nickname when we were ten years old. You'd think people would have forgotten it by now. Except they couldn't, because I hadn't let them forget it. For years I'd been eager to hurt Velma, to lash out and make her feel the same pain I'd felt when my family fell apart. It was the same pain I'd felt until recently, only sometimes I *did* still feel it, even though things were so much better now.

The truth was, I'd gone scorched earth on my best friend, and I was still paying for it. So was she.

I squeezed her hand. "Those girls are almost always wrong, you know. Half the time they just make up gossip out of thin air."

Velma put on a brave, knowing smile. "But half the time they don't."

I didn't have a response to that. It was true that occasionally Aimee and Aparna got their stories right. But I couldn't imagine Shaggy asking Fred to keep Velma, one of his oldest friends, away from him. And I didn't want to imagine Fred agreeing to it.

Unless, of course, Shaggy's secret was so massive, he would put up every roadblock he could find to prevent us from finding it.

"We know Shaggy's probably in his dad's study," I said. "So let's decide right now: What's our priority question?"

Velma stared at the black-and-white tile floor. I knew which question I wanted to get to the bottom of first, but I wasn't sure where her head was at. Especially now, after that dance with Fred, and her mistake with the fake jewels.

Finally, she set her jaw and gave me a steely look. Decisive Velma was the one I knew best.

DAPHNE

"Shaggy's our friend. He's our priority."

I nodded once and together we crept out of the bathroom, down the hall, and straight to the war room.

"One," Velma whispered as we stood outside the door. Warm light cast a glow on our feet.

"Two," I counted. "Three!"

I opened the knob and pushed hard. Velma followed me inside.

"Shaggy Rogers!" I said. "We're your friends, and we're here to help!"

"We know something's up with you, and we're not leaving until you tell us what it is!" Velma stated. We stood in twin Wonder Woman poses, hands on hips, feet spread apart. For a moment I actually *felt* like a superhero. I gotta say, I didn't hate it.

Shaggy stood in the center of the war room, with Jack at his side. They both whipped their heads around at our arrival. Jack looked dismayed to see us, but Shaggy looked relieved.

"Like . . . something is definitely up!" Shaggy pointed to the wall above his father's oversized mahogany desk.

I looked up. The walls of Mr. Rogers's study were crammed with items: photos, memorabilia, framed American flags; candelabras, medallions, newspaper clippings. And right there, in the space directly above Mr. Rogers's desk, was a gaping hole where something large had been. Remnants of it remained—a shadow on the wallpaper where the sun had lightened its colors; a ring of dust.

"It's gone," Jack said. His voice was awed, subdued.

"What is?" Velma asked. I tried to place what could have been there, tried to recall if I'd ever taken note of that space during the handful of times I'd been in this room.

Suddenly, a memory: a sleepover during the summer of Mystery Inc. The four of us had split up to play a game we coined called hide-and-scare—a game with an obvious goal—and Shaggy and I were the first to hide. It was one of the many times his dad was traveling, and I convinced him to bring me here, to the war room, where I knew the perfect place to hide from Velma and Fred. Giggling and shushing each other, Shaggy and I ducked behind the suit of armor that stood, hulking, in the corner of the room. We stayed there for enough time that I began to memorize the walls, counting the artifacts and whispering my questions about them to Shaggy. He knew everything about every item in that room; he'd told me once that his dad used to quiz him on Rogers family history.

"I know what's missing," I announced. Shaggy's eyes glistened with sadness. He nodded glumly.

"Can someone tell me already?" Velma pleaded.

I checked with Shaggy; he nodded. I took a deep breath. "The Crystal Cove Crystal."

DAPHNE

A hush fell over the room. For the first time I could ever remember, laid-back, chill Shaggy looked like he might burst into tears. "Someone stole my father's, like, most prized possession."

A famous—or infamous—artifact, the Crystal Cove Crystal was a shining, craggy gemstone about the size of a dinner plate that was discovered hundreds of years ago in the sea caves by an ancestor of the Rogers family, one of the original settlers of Crystal Cove. Deep purple in color with threads of shiny yellow running through it, the crystal was well known around town—my own mother had even included purple stones as a central theme in *The Curse of Crystal Cove*. Decades ago, someone had dubbed its rich, thick color "Crystal Cove Purple," and, like most things surrounding this place, there were a few conflicting stories about it.

Some people said the Crystal had once been much larger, but that various Rogers family members, who had passed down the Crystal through each generation, had sold off bits and pieces of it throughout the years to finance various business deals . . . or, depending on who you asked, to pay off illicit debts. But the Rogers family had always maintained that the item they possessed was original and had never been tampered with; instead, they claimed, they had protected it. To hear them tell it, the Crystal Cove Crystal was so vital to the history of this town that only a Rogers could keep it safe. It had sat in a custom-built case on a custom-built shelf in Mr. Rogers's study for as long as I'd known Shaggy. According to scientists, no other gem like it had yet been discovered elsewhere in the world.

And according to legend, it had mystical powers.

"How long has the Crystal been missing?" Velma asked the room. For a long while, no one said anything. "Shaggy? How long?"

Shaggy shook himself, like he was waking himself up from a long nap. Somehow, even in the warm light of the study, he looked wan, washed out. Paler than usual and more tired than I'd ever seen him.

"Hard to say. My mom, like, never comes in here, and I haven't been in this room in a couple of weeks. There was that one time when Taylor was over and I was giving her a tour of the house."

"When's the last time your dad was here?" I asked, doing the math.

Shaggy shrugged. "My dad and I are, like, two snacks on the opposite side of the buffet table. We barely see each other. He was away all last week, right?"

Jack nodded, and Shaggy continued, "He flew back late Friday and went straight to my parents' master bedroom on the first floor. Scooby and I were up watching a movie, and I, like, for sure would've heard him if he were upstairs.

DAPHNE

I even peeked in here to see, but it was empty. And the Crystal was still here."

"What about Saturday?" I prompted.

Shaggy scratched his head, thinking. "My mom had pulled a thirty-six-hour shift, so she went on duty first thing in the morning. My dad . . . he went straight to his office downtown that morning. I know 'cause he gave me and Scooby a ride. He was supposed to meet my mom for lunch, but then the thing at the beach happened and . . . like, they never got to eat. Then he flew out again Saturday afternoon."

"So no one's been in here since late Friday night?"

Shaggy looked at the ceiling as if the answer were pasted on the chandelier. Finally, he said, "Probably not. The house-keepers aren't really allowed in here. One too many incidents in the past of misplaced papers from my dad's desk."

I could see Mr. Rogers getting really mad about some-one touching his stuff. Apparently Jack could, too, because he put an arm around his cousin and said, "Oh man. Oh, Shaggy. Your dad is going to be furious."

Shaggy closed his eyes, his shoulders drooping even more than usual. "Yeah."

"And your house has an alarm system, right?" I confirmed.

"Yeah. It's only on at night, though."

Velma sighed. "In a house this big?"

Shaggy grew defensive. "It's Crystal Cove. Our home. No one would break in here. Everyone knows us!"

"And they also probably know when you're home, and when you're not," I pointed out.

"I'm, like, beyond furious. We're talking about extreme rage." Jack was still talking about Mr. Rogers, pacing around the room with his arms crossed.

"Probably," Shaggy whispered. I felt so bad for Shaggy just then. I'd done some really rotten things to my mom over the years, but I'd never felt the kind of fear about her reaction to my behavior that he was displaying.

"We need to narrow down the window of time when someone could have gotten into your house, snuck into this room, and taken the Crystal without anyone seeing them," Velma said.

"No one was here Saturday morning." Shaggy said it decisively. I wanted to scream at him, *We know! We know because we were following you Saturday morning!* But obviously, I didn't.

"Let's call your mom," Velma suggested.

"Man," Jack repeated. I glared at him but he kept going. "He leaves you home alone and this happens? Yikes, bro. Yikes."

"Okay," I interrupted, a ping in my stomach reminding me to talk to Velma later about who this Jack character was. "No sense in scaring Shaggy to death. Shaggy, call your mom."

DAPHNE

Jack whistled. Shaggy sniffled. And Velma and I stared at each other, daring each other to voice out loud what we were thinking.

Finally, she caved. "Can I just raise a possibility for a sec? What if . . ."

Shaggy looked interested. "What is it?"

Velma chewed her lip. "Well, isn't it just a little suspicious? Your dad's prized possession, the most famous item in Crystal Cove, goes missing at the same exact time a bunch of mysterious jewels wash up onshore?"

"This house is about as far away from the beach as you can get and still be in Crystal Cove," I pointed out. My heart was doing that thing again where it was beating so hard, it echoed in my ears. "And your dad's travel schedule is pretty reliable . . ."

"And your mom's work schedule is public information . . ." Velma added.

"I don't get it," Jack said flatly.

But understanding was dawning on Shaggy's face. "You think the jewels were a distraction?"

"A diversion," Velma clarified.

"So . . . it's not a coincidence that the jewels washed up on Saturday, the same day my dad's crystal disappeared."

Velma shook her head. "Definitely not a coincidence. More like an intentional, strategic tactic."

"Someone unloaded something enticing enough to

capture everyone in town's attention for a couple of hours," I said, knowing even as I said it that it was true, that we were finally—finally!—onto something. "And in that time, your house was empty."

"And everyone was rushing to the beach," said Shaggy, eyes darting between me and Velma, beginning to look scared.

"And once everyone was out of the way, the Crystal Cove Crystal was fair game. Unprotected."

"So the jewels themselves are . . . practically meaningless!" Velma snapped her fingers. She had that look on her face, the one that said *Gotcha!* The one that said *Now I get it.* It mirrored the feeling swirling inside my stomach: the understanding that this was finally a lead, a plausible answer. A path forward. And, in a way, a whole new mystery to solve: Who stole the Crystal?

"The jewels were a ploy," I confirmed, feeling the enormity of what was unfolding before us. "Someone was after the Crystal Cove Crystal all along."

Velma nodded. "Looks like we've got another case to crack."

The hooded figure stays close to the shadows. Soon, it will be morning. But for now, the darkness stretches far and wide, blanketing Crystal Cove with a hush.

A heavy thing, this famous Crystal. The hooded figure hadn't realized just how heavy it would be, how awkward to carry. A few times, it almost tumbles onto the street. Still, it's held tight, close to the chest, its power seeping through the soft, protective cloth around it.

Snap.

What was that? The figure pauses, heart thrashing. The Crystal's final destination is so close.

Creeping through the night, the hooded figure feels a warming inside their own chest, where the Crystal is nestled. Ducking around a corner shaded by trees, the figure pauses, considers. From underneath the cloth the Crystal seems to light up, to pulse with power. It glows.

"We're almost home," the figure whispers, stroking it. So many stories this stone has to tell. So many lessons. Maybe now, finally, they can be free.

The Crystal hasn't seen the light of day in who knows how long. Generations, maybe. Years, at least. Samuel Rogers had defied every known theory about the Crystal by tacking it up on his wall, like he owned it. Like it belonged to him.

The hooded figure burns at the thought. The Crystal belongs to no one, and to everyone. It never should have been removed from its birthplace to begin with. Look at what's happened since then. This town has borne witness to so many mysterious occurrences, so many catastrophes. Can you call that a coincidence?

No, the figure knows. You could not.

Crack.

A pause; the figure takes inventory of the night.

There is someone else out there.

Taking off down the street, and another, and then another. Running away from the chase, the darkness.

The carefully laid plans will have to be altered, the figure realizes, deciding to change course.

Now home, reckless with adrenaline, the hooded figure drops to the floor, knees banging on wood, laughing and crying in silence.

Soon, the Crystal Cove Crystal will be in its proper home. And the ancestors can rest.

VELMA

BY MIDDAY THE NEXT day, the news was all over town. The rumors that had run rampant for days—about how the Vanished were sending messages, or maybe even returning to claim the land that had been stolen from them; about how the Lady Vampire of the Bay was back, terrorizing the people of Crystal Cove—morphed into something even more sinister: Crystal Cove was under attack from dark forces.

And the *Howler*'s latest headline definitely wasn't helping tamp down the climate of fear that had overtaken the town.

I dropped my phone, disgusted, faceup on the table in front of Daphne. She didn't even glance at it; she already knew what it said.

She sighed and pushed away her lunch. "I know. It's not great."

"'The Curse of Crystal Cove Continues as Town's Most Important Artifact Vanishes'?" I said, fuming. "Is Milford *trying* to give people heart attacks?"

"I'm just an intern," she reminded me. I dropped into the seat next to her and pulled out my bagged lunch. She eyed my sad little sandwich before pushing her own tray over. "Sushi?"

"I don't want sushi; I want answers."

"We'll get them," Daphne assured me. Her brow crinkled. "I think."

"We need a new plan." I took a deep breath. "And . . . maybe we should tell Shaggy's mom about the ruby we found in the Haunted Village."

Daphne shook her head. "Let's keep that to ourselves a while longer. The police are investigating the theft of the Crystal Cove Crystal," she said. "Shaggy told me they're reviewing video logs from the Rogerses' security cameras right now."

"He also told us those videos auto-delete after forty-eight hours," I reminded her. We went back and forth for a few minutes, trading barbs about how—or whether—the police would investigate, and whether it would prove worthwhile. The way I saw it, the police hadn't bothered to do even a cursory investigation into the jewels, and they probably didn't see the connection between them and the Crystal.

But I did.

"Hey." Shaggy appeared, sliding over an empty chair and collapsing into it. His tall, lanky body made a C-shape as he slumped over and rested his head on the lunch table. Daphne and I exchanged worried glances.

"You okay?" Daphne asked him.

He moaned in response.

She pushed her plate over to him. "Sushi?"

"Nobody wants your day-old sushi, Daph," I snapped.

An incredulous expression crossed her face. "Do you honestly think I would eat day-old sushi? That's harsh, V."

"My dad is going to murder me," Shaggy said, lifting his head and reaching for Daphne's plate. "I may as well die from food poisoning first."

"What's the latest?" I was eager to hear some truth straight from the source. No one at school could be trusted, and of course, neither could the *Howler*.

Shaggy filled us in. His mom's police squad was investigating, and the Rogerses were fully cooperating; nothing else appeared to be missing from their house—not even their expensive jewelry or electronic equipment; not even the big wad of cash they kept in an empty coffee canister on the kitchen counter for emergencies. So far, there was no sign of a physical break-in, but the cops were still looking for evidence. As far as Shaggy knew, there were no official leads. Shaggy hadn't talked to his dad, but his mom had—Mr. Rogers was on his way home from his latest trip and, so far, he'd ignored every one of Shaggy's apologetic text messages.

"You know it's not your fault, right?" Daphne peered into his face.

"I know. And, like, I'm sure my dad knows, too. But I was the only one home. And, like, my dad and me . . ." Shaggy's voice trailed off.

Few people understood weird family dynamics as well as I did. If someone were to ask me what was up with my dad, I wasn't sure I'd be able to adequately convey it to them. But Shaggy and his dad, at that moment, seemed like a problem way out of my league. It was hard enough to penetrate Shaggy's oh-so-carefully-cultivated surfer shell; no way could I crack the hard, cold nut that was Mr. Rogers, too. At least, not without a whole lot more time and resources at my disposal.

"Okay, we have a few minutes left until sixth period," Daphne said, pulling out her little reporter's notebook and pen. I tried to refrain from rolling my eyes, but I confess I was not particularly successful. "Let's figure out who would even want the Crystal Cove Crystal. Like, pie-in-the-sky, throw-anything-at-the-wall ideas."

I nodded. "Good plan. I have a few ideas. Anyone you're thinking about?"

Daphne nodded. "Yep. Taylor Burnett."

Shaggy nearly jumped out of his chair. "No way! Like, why would you say that?"

"She's kind of odd, Shag," Daphne said. "Something about the way she's always watching people . . . I don't know, I just get a vibe from her."

"Rude." Shaggy crossed his arms. "Taylor's a sweet kid, she's just, like, going through a hard time. I've known her since she was a baby."

"Well, tell her to stop staring at everybody all the time. Maybe then she'll find some friends."

"She has found some friends," he pointed out, jabbing himself in the chest with his thumb. "Me."

Daphne raised an eyebrow. "Why are you so intent on protecting her?"

"Why are you so intent on, like, calling her out?" He shook his head. "She's just a kid, Daph. I told her mom I'd watch out for her. What do you care?"

I gave Daphne a look. Now wasn't the time to tell Shaggy about how we might've spotted his old friend lurking around the Haunted Village. "Let's move on." I drummed my fingers on the table and said the first thing that popped into my head. "What about Jack?"

"Like, what?" Shaggy guffawed. "My cousin?"

"Like Daphne said. Anything at the wall. He shows up out of the blue the day before the Crystal disappears? It's suspicious!" I argued. "I've never even heard you mention Jack."

"Like, you've never heard me talk about anything but Scooby, surfing, and pizza," Shaggy muttered.

"Whoa." I held up my hands in surrender. "Don't blame me because you like to keep things surface-level. I've tried to be your friend. Your *real* friend."

"Why don't we all take a breath," Daphne suggested. Her voice had that bright tint to it, but I could see she was alarmed.

Shaggy shook his head. "This is pointless. It's not like you two are gonna be able to solve this."

"Hey," Daphne protested while I stewed. I wanted to scoop up the remaining bites of sushi and throw them in Shaggy's face. "Do I need to remind you, it was Velma and me who found Marcy and everyone else? We solved the kidnapping mystery!"

"Not to mention a ton of other cases when we were kids," I said, disgusted to hear a wobble in my voice.

"Exactly," Shaggy said icily. "*Kids.*"

Daphne pointed a finger at Shaggy. "You need to chill out."

He stared at her, looking like he was going to say something. Finally, he sighed, and her face softened. Something happened between the two of them, a moment I couldn't define.

"You're right," he said quietly. To me, he said, "Sorry, Velma. I'm, like, wound a little tight right now."

"Me too," I mumbled.

Shaggy put his head in his hands again. He looked so forlorn, so completely down, that I felt a rush of desperation to help him. And there was only one way I could think of to do so.

Gently, I circled back to our earlier conversation. "I'd like to cross your cousin off the list of potential suspects. I really would. I just need you to give me a reason why."

I held my breath, but to my surprise, Shaggy nodded, his face serious. "Well, for starters, he's a Rogers. I'm not sure why he'd feel the need to, like, *steal* the Crystal. It already belongs to him, right?"

Daphne nodded. "Sure. But he's also a stranger—" As Shaggy's eyebrows leapt to his hairline, Daphne held up her hand. "To us, he's a stranger. So we need to clear him using all the regular tactics we would use to clear any other suspect."

Shaggy shook his head but laid out his defense. "Jack slept in the guest house Friday night, and then he spent all of Saturday morning at the office with my dad. Like, I get it, but I don't think he ever had an opportunity to take the Crystal."

"Cool," I said smoothly as Daphne drew a line through his name, knowing that she was just doing it for show. In actuality, both Jack and Taylor were very much still *on* the list. "So he's off the list. Who's next?"

We were all silent for a moment, thinking. Shaggy started to get that nervous look on his face, the one where his left eyebrow twitches, and he moved around in his seat a bit. He was tall, Shaggy, and these lunch chairs were tiny. But he'd managed to sit still so far, until now.

"Say it," I suggested. Okay, *commanded*. Semantics.

"I mean . . ."

"Who's got a motive?" Daphne pressed. "Any motive. Large or small, silly or smart. We have to explore them all."

"Like, my dad is a guy with a lot going on. Lots of balls up in the air!" Shaggy barked a nervous laugh.

"He's been pretty stressed lately," I said, thinking of the last time I'd seen him. And *every* time I'd seen him. He wore his stress like a sweater, Mr. Rogers—heavy and unmistakable.

"My dad? He's, like, ninety-seven percent composed of stress!"

"Any new stressors? Has he done anything out of the ordinary?" Daphne's pen was poised over her notebook.

"Gambling debts? Insurance fraud?" I suggested.

"Velma," Daphne hissed.

"What? We have to go through all these possibilities." I crossed my arms.

"He's been traveling more than usual, I guess," Shaggy

VELMA

said. He crossed one ankle over his knee, nearly knocking over the lunch table. He was making *me* nervous. "But that's normal when your biggest company is about to go under. Also, my grandma's been sick, so I know he's visited her a few times."

"Did you say . . . your dad's biggest company is about to go under? Rogers Enterprises?"

"Uhhh . . ." Shaggy rubbed his head. When he pulled his hand away, his hair stuck up in three new places. "I, like . . ."

"Come on, Shag," Daphne coaxed, her voice soft, pleading.

"Like . . . my dad has a ton of companies. Some, like, flourish, but some explode and collapse into pieces." He shrugged, looking down at the table, his knee jostling. "Listen, his business is not my business, you know what I mean?"

"But it could be *our* business," I said.

"The Crystal is worth a lot of money to some people," Daphne mused.

"Maybe enough to save an underperforming business?" I held my breath as my words landed. I was sure Shaggy would freak out at the implication that his dad had something to do with the missing Crystal.

But instead of anger, Shaggy radiated fear. "Like, please. I'm begging you. I'm not even supposed to know about that. I just overheard him a couple weeks ago, on the phone. And then I saw some paperwork I wasn't supposed to see. Please. Like . . . just, please. Don't say anything to anyone. A rumor like this would make it even worse."

"We have to look into every and any lead," Daphne explained. She placed her hand over Shaggy's, but then quickly removed it. For the second time, they seemed to have an unspoken conversation, right in front of me, and I was bewildered. I knew Daphne had *technically* spent a lot more time with Shaggy over the years—his parties, Fred's house after school, all the stuff the in-crowd did together—but I suddenly realized how all those years I'd chosen to keep to myself had had consequences. I'd missed a lot.

"Please," he repeated. "I don't think my mom knows about this. She'd be so worried. And she has enough to worry about."

"I'm sure she does." Daphne squeezed his hand. "But shouldn't your dad be honest? If he wants a real investigation, he'll need to disclose stuff like this. All of it."

"It's just that . . . well, my dad has a reputation to uphold," Shaggy said softly, his eyes only on Daphne's. I started to get that invisible feeling again, that sensation that everyone else around me was real while I was just a ghost, just a shadow of a girl. "I don't do the best job of that for him. Jack does, though. He's like . . . like the son I'm sure my dad wishes I were."

VELMA

I closed my eyes and took a breath. Shaggy's pain was palpable.

"I'm sure that's not true," Daphne murmured. Her eyes got a faraway look. "But believe me. I know what it's like to feel like you're not living up to your parents' ideas of who you should be. I get it."

I stared at my feet. My combat boots were scuffed; one lace was untied. I concentrated really hard on that lace, on counting its knots and bumps, trying to sort out this rising tide of emotions.

I had always wondered if Shaggy was deeper than he led everyone to believe he was. And of course, I knew now that Daphne certainly was. I just wasn't sure why we were doing all that hiding. And I couldn't help but wonder what kinds of things everyone else around us was hiding, and if maybe we'd all be better off revealing ourselves once and for all.

DAPHNE

THE *HOWLER* OFFICES WERE humming when I arrived after school. I felt like I was visibly drooping, Shaggy's emotions still weighing me down. It was heavy, thinking about what Shaggy was going through, and knowing what I knew of his dad made me all the more worried for him. By the time I sat down at my desk, I was more determined than ever to help my friend.

Because that's what Shaggy was, I reminded myself, despite those few strange seconds we'd experienced at lunch that day: a friend. And when I saw Ram approaching our cube, I was reminded of that even more.

He grinned widely when he saw me and, *poof,* all thoughts of Shaggy fell away. Well, kind of. Those weird thoughts, anyway.

DAPHNE

"I need your help," I said before Ram even sat down. My stomach tingled.

"Sounds serious, Blake."

"Super." I surveyed the two conference rooms that sat at either end of our floor. Both were filled with people.

"Maybe now's a good time to grab that coffee?" Ram suggested, and I nodded even as my heart sank. An afternoon coffee break wasn't exactly what I'd had in mind for our first date, but it would have to do. And besides, I still wasn't sure if it even *was* a date.

We took the elevator to the cafeteria on the top floor of the building. The coffee was free for all building employees, so I didn't even have to worry about who would pay for it (hey, I'll take the wins where I can get them these days) and we quickly poured our own cups and settled into a quiet section of the caf, overlooking the parking lot in the back. *Romantic.*

"You know I got that headline changed, right?" Ram said.

It took me a beat to recall what he meant. The headline about all signs pointing to the Vanished returning felt like months ago; years ago. I'd barely noticed the change, and besides, once we discovered the Crystal was the real story, Milton had pivoted quickly. Today's headline was slightly calmer but no less compelling: *Duped! Town Discovers Infamous, Historic Crystal Is Missing as Reports*

Confirm the Washed-Up Jewels Are a Diversion.

"Right," I said hurriedly. Then, remembering my end goal—and my assets—I flashed him my best smile. "Actually, that's kind of what I wanted to check in with you about."

"My headline?"

"Close. More like . . . your ace sleuthing skills." (*And your ace Milford skills*, I wanted to add.) I took a steaming sip while maintaining eye contact. I hoped I looked alluring, but it's possible I just looked dumb. "Obviously, the police are now focusing on finding the Crystal."

"The police and the rest of this legend-obsessed town, yeah." Ram leaned back in his seat and rested his feet on the empty chair between us. "Did you see the latest police log? Someone said they saw a giant crystal hovering over the beach around midnight."

"That sounds about right," I said. I'd already seen a couple of new rumors on my social media feeds overnight, too. Sammie Daniels had texted our group to say she and her family were so scared, they were planning on getting out of town as, according to her, "ghosts were not on the Daniels family agenda." "Milford must be all over this story, too, right?"

"He's the most single-minded man I've ever met." Ram shook his head. "I've been here since my morning classes ended, and it's the only thing he's talked about. Well, that and whether our latest video about the Vanished has gone viral or not."

"Web traffic must be high, huh?"

"Through the roof, according to my buddies in the digital department. Every article about the jewels, whether it's focused on the Vanished or ghosts or whatever, has smashed our previous records. This is the kind of stuff Milford lives for."

I took another sip while I pondered that. Milford was definitely on my list of suspects—top of it, actually, with his name on the first line in my notebook—but I remembered that Velma had thought he might be involved in Marcy's disappearance in our previous case, and instead he'd come through for us when we needed help. After that experience, I wasn't convinced he'd steal the Crystal just for a good story. Especially now that I had confirmation the articles about the washed-up jewels were performing so well. Milford had no motive, as far as I could tell.

Except for the fact that he seemed to hate Mr. Rogers, of course. I wished Velma and I had asked Shaggy about their backstory this morning. I made a mental note to mention it the next time I saw Shaggy.

In the meantime, I hurriedly steered the conversation to where I needed it to go. "What do you know about the Rogers family?"

"Other than they run every business in town?" Ram shrugged. Today he wore a green-and-white striped sweater that nicely complemented his orange sneakers. "I've seen your friend around town a bit. He and his dog are hard to miss."

"Yeah, the Rogerses are Crystal Cove royalty," I confirmed. "And a Rogers was the only surviving settler, after the Vanishing. But what do you know about Mr. Rogers, specifically?"

Ram shrugged again. He was losing interest, I could tell. I straightened my posture, recrossed my legs, and licked my lips. *Focus, Blake.* "I hope you don't mind, but I googled you."

Ram's head jerked up. I felt a snake of satisfaction curl up my stomach.

"I noticed your last internship was at the *San Francisco Financial Journal*, is that right?"

"That's right." Ram smiled, like he was glad I'd looked into him. "Mostly financial reporting, with occasional forays into some juicy Wall Street stuff. Why?"

I maintained Ram's gaze for a few moments without saying anything. It was a little trick I'd learned a long time ago—keeping silent, a hint of a smile on your lips, made people think you knew more than you actually did.

He leaned forward, nearly knocking over his cup. "I know that look, Blake."

DAPHNE

I let my smile widen a bit more, just enough so that he knew I knew.

"That's the look of a reporter with a hunch."

My grin burst open at that, and the best part was, it was genuine. Ram didn't think of me as some little high school intern. I was a reporter. *We* were reporters.

"Not a hunch, exactly," I clarified. "More like the potential for a hunch. And I think you're just the guy to handle it."

Ram's eyes bored into mine, warm and inviting. "I'm listening."

For a moment, the background noise of the cafeteria faded away. I hesitated. My brain knew I was sitting in the *Howler* offices in Crystal Cove, but I had the distinct impression I was standing on a cliff, and I had to make a decision about whether to jump off and fly . . . or back up and walk away.

For the first time I could remember, I wanted to jump. I just felt like, finally, someone would actually catch me.

* * *

When I called Velma that night, her voice crackled through the phone—a bad connection, which meant she was in the Dinkleys' new-old house. That whole area had been a dead zone for cell service my entire life.

"So what's the latest on the reporting front?" she asked.

"Well, for starters, the police didn't find anything on

the Rogerses' security cameras," I filled her in as I sat at my desk and clicked around the internet. One of Milford's top reporters had finally met with the police to get the latest status of the investigation, so I was brimming with updates.

"Which we expected."

"But still, a bummer," I continued. "All the house staff have been interviewed, but so far, no one seems to have any motive, and they all have alibis. The locks on all the doors were working normally, none of the windows were broken or anything like that, and other than the Crystal, not a speck was out of place."

"What about fingerprints?"

"They've dusted," I confirmed. For a moment I lost my train of thought—somehow, I'd ended up on Hartwood University's website, where a massive photo of Ram's face stared back at me from their home page, those dark eyes smiling. (Clearly, Hartwood's marketing department had also noticed how, er, attractive Ram's appearance would be to prospective students.) "But so far nothing's really turned up. The cleaners dust the whole house every week, except for Mr. Rogers's study. If the thief touched anything in there, they must've worn gloves."

"Still," Velma wondered. "I can't believe there's nothing unusual."

"We really only have one angle to go on here."

DAPHNE

I could practically hear Velma nodding. "Shaggy's not going to like that."

I felt myself deflate a little—I didn't want to hurt Shaggy. But, I reminded myself, the best way—the only way—to help him was to solve the case. Once the Crystal was found, Shaggy and his dad could sort out whatever family issues they had. And then I remembered: I had a plan. And I was staring right at him. I mean, it.

"Here's the problem," I said, sending a wish up into the universe that Velma would hear me out as I closed my laptop. "There's no way the Rogers family is going to let us anywhere near their financials."

"We'll have to keep it on the sly. If the wrong people start to catch on to our investigation . . ."

"Exactly," I said. I plopped onto my bed and stared at the ceiling. "But . . ."

"Daphne . . ." Velma warned through the crackles of the phone.

"Well, what if I know someone who really gets this stuff? Who, I don't know, maybe worked as a financial reporter?"

"We are absolutely not partnering with Ram on this case." Velma's voice was flat. I decided to pretend it was just a bad connection.

"How did you know I was talking about Ram?!"

"You're pretty much always talking about Ram."

Well, that stung. And it was so not true. I forged ahead, spilling my plan in one breath. "Velma-hear-me-out. He's-a-skilled-reporter-and-specializes-in-financial-reporting. Since-no-one-in-Crystal-Cove-really-knows-him-he-can-be-more-inconspicious-than-either-of-us-can. And-with-his-university-credentials-he-has-access-to-way-more-resources-than-we-do!"

Silence. As I caught my breath, I absentmindedly wandered over to my closet, flipping through the hangers until I found the dress I was looking for. It was a trendy cut, but it was a deep forest green, not a color I normally wore. My mom had bought it for me on one of her many travels, back before we'd really been on speaking terms and she used to try to purchase my love. But Ram's green-and-white sweater had reminded me of it. I fingered the soft fabric, the belt that cinched in the waist. He was such a sharp dresser; I thought maybe it was time I upped my game.

"You there?" I said when I couldn't take the silence any longer.

She sighed. And, if you asked me, surrendered. "I'm here."

"So are you good with this plan? Because . . . well . . . I kind of already asked him to partner with us. And, well . . ."

"Oh, jeepers, what now?" Velma sputtered. I heard a crash, and then Velma shouted, "Ow!"

"You okay?"

DAPHNE

"I just tripped."

"What are you doing, anyway?"

Another bump, and then Velma's muffled voice said, "Cleaning. My parents moved a bunch of boxes into the house, so I thought I'd get started on the kitchen."

I wrinkled my nose, remembering the state of the Dinkleys' new-old kitchen. "Do you want me to come over?"

"Honestly? Yes. But don't. It's getting late, and I'm leaving soon anyway."

"Okay. But just say the word, and I will."

"I know you will. That's the only reason I'm not mad about you already asking Ram to help us out."

"Um . . . about that." I chewed on my lip while Velma's huff came through the phone.

"Okay, seriously, Daph? I can't take any more. Spill it. All of it."

"The thing is . . . Ram already found some stuff. And it's big."

Silence. And then, Velma's voice, clear as day. "Come over. Now. And bring Ram with you. And maybe Shaggy, too." And then, wearily: "I'll call for pizza."

* * *

"You sure this is the right place?"

"Oh, I'm sure."

Ram blinked in the darkness as we trudged up the back hill to the Dinkley house. By the time I'd gathered him

191

and called Shaggy and persuaded him to meet us at Velma's—with promises of a great story (for Ram) and lots of food (for Shaggy)—darkness had fully fallen. The Dinkley house, with its peeling paint and old, sloping roof, looked like a movie set. An abandoned, haunted movie set. A shiver ran down my spine—from the cool wind whipping over the Dinkley lot or from the presence of Ram, I wasn't sure.

When we knocked on the back door, Shaggy opened it, Scooby right on his heels. His face fell when he saw us. "Aw, man, I thought you'd be pizza."

Velma's face popped up behind Shaggy's shoulder. I started, suddenly remembering she was wearing contacts. Would I ever think of Velma without her glasses? "Come in, guys. Shaggy, pizza's coming, I promise."

She ushered us inside and, just as we all got settled at the kitchen table—I noticed someone had wiped it, so most of the dust was gone at least—the front doorbell rang and Shaggy raced to answer it. I seized my opportunity.

"Velma, Shaggy's probably not going to like what Ram found," I whispered urgently, eyes darting to the swinging kitchen door. "So let's be gentle with him, okay?"

"Why do you think I wouldn't be gentle with him?" she asked, frowning.

"I'm just saying," I pressed. "You have a tendency to be a little . . ."

Velma narrowed her eyes at me. I smiled and shrugged in response. "Blunt. And we love you for it."

"Who do we love, and why?" Shaggy asked. He'd reappeared at the kitchen door, carrying two large pies—one for him, one for the rest of us—and I swear, I've never seen him so happy. No wonder Shaggy never had romantic relationships, I mused as he carefully placed the boxes on the table and opened one up, steam clouding the room. No person could ever compare to the love he had for food. Or his dog, I realized, watching him lovingly cut half a slice for Scooby.

I made introductions and small talk while we ate and then, just when Shaggy had stuffed half a piece into his mouth, I did what we'd come here for.

"So, Shaggy, we have some news."

He paused mid-chew, his eyes darting between me and Velma, who dove in. "Ram works at the *Howler* with Daphne, but he's actually done financial reporting before, at an internship he did last summer break. So he has some experience digging into companies' public records and uncovering the secrets they're trying to hide."

Shaggy swallowed. "Like, okay. Cool, I guess."

As gingerly as I could, I broke the news. "And he's uncovered some stuff about Rogers Enterprises that we think you should hear from us first, before it's public."

Shaggy kept looking back and forth between me and Velma, almost like he was deliberately pretending Ram wasn't in the room. The air was charged with a nervous energy. And yet there was something behind Shaggy's eyes that told me maybe he wasn't going to be as surprised by the news as we'd feared.

"First, you should know the Crystal is valued at an impressively high price," Ram said, dropping his slice on his plate and opening the reporter's notebook he'd pulled out of his jacket pocket. He flipped a page. "Your dad had the Crystal reassessed about three months ago, and according to what I could find, its value has skyrocketed over the past few years. And your dad renewed the insurance policy just last month."

He held up his notebook and showed Shaggy the numbers he'd jotted down. Shaggy's eyes nearly bugged out. So did Velma's, and I knew right away what she must be thinking: Was this a classic case of insurance fraud, where someone gets a premium policy on an expensive item only to report it stolen later so they can cash in?

"So with that background knowledge, here's what's important." Ram flipped to another page. "Rogers Enterprises is a massive business, with full ownership of about a half dozen companies and holdings in lots of others. Your dad has a hand in all sorts of industries—clothing and beverage, insurance and textiles, a real mix of stuff. Which is smart. But based on my research, there are

DAPHNE

some inconsistencies in the reported earnings for Rogers Enterprises and its actual wealth."

Shaggy closed the lid to the near-empty pizza box. He sighed uncharacteristically. "Like, inconsistencies?"

Ram nodded. "Over the past year, at least according to the documents I've found, most of the Rogers-branded companies have become insolvent."

Shaggy blinked.

"Tell them what that means, exactly," I murmured to Ram. I wanted him to say the words out loud, mostly because he'd been the one to discover it . . . and partly because I thought it would hurt Shaggy too much if I delivered them.

"May I be direct?" Ram's voice was kind, soft. Shaggy paused, and then nodded. "This means that, on paper, Rogers Enterprises is . . . well, in the red. Underwater. Broke, basically."

Shaggy stared at the floor. He had one long leg crossed over so that his ankle was resting on his knee, and it shook like a machine, knocking into the table with a consistent beat. Even Scooby, sensing the tension in the room, cocked his head and stared at Ram. I concentrated on the table, on the drips of sauce Shaggy had spilled.

"Do you think . . ." Shaggy said, breaking the awkward silence. "I mean, like, is my dad . . . ?"

"We don't know if this is related at all to the Crystal, or

to the jewels," I rushed to clarify. I reached out my hand to grab Shaggy's, but something stopped me, and I awkwardly retreated. I cleared my throat. "It just means there's a motive, maybe."

"Or, at the very least, it means your dad is probably a lot more stressed than any of us realized," Velma added.

"If the police are doing their job right, this information will come to light eventually," Ram explained. "And then . . . it'll be chaos for your family. I'm really sorry, man."

"Like, yikes," Shaggy said. His sandy hair seemed to have grown another inch since I'd last seen him at school that day and he brushed it out of his eyes, which were wide and round and wet. "I knew something was up . . ."

We waited for a minute to see if he would finish the thought, but when he didn't, Velma jumped in. "Like what?" she asked.

Shaggy cast his eyes up at the ceiling, and then down at the floor, and then uncrossed his legs. The table stopped shaking. Finally, he said, "Jack's visit. It was unexpected. And it sent up a red flag for me."

"You think Jack has something to do with this?" Velma prompted, leaning forward.

"I don't think he's directly involved. Like, no way." Shaggy looked aghast. "He'd tell me. For sure he'd tell me. But . . . I wouldn't put it past my dad to use Jack somehow. Like, without Jack knowing."

We were all silent then, listening to the wind whip around the corners of the back porch, whistling in through the small window over the sink that Velma must have opened.

"Listen." Shaggy suddenly straightened up, meeting our eyes directly. "This, like, stays between us, right?"

"Of course," I said.

"Definitely," Velma added. I looked at Ram, waiting for his confirmation, but he was busy jotting something in his notebook.

While the silence settled, I tried to recount the possibilities behind what Ram had discovered. Was it possible that Mr. Rogers was in such dire financial straits that he would sell off his beloved Crystal Cove Crystal to the highest bidder and then set it up to look like a robbery so he could ultimately cash a sweet check and save his businesses? But would he *really* do that? The Crystal Cove Crystal was iconic. Meaningful. Irreplaceable. Especially to the Rogers family, with all their talk of town legacy and family history.

I thought of what I knew about Shaggy's dad—his harsh demeanor, the way he was always too busy working to ever attend our school events or Shaggy's surf competitions, the disappointed way he always looked at his son.

And then I thought about all the things I didn't know about Shaggy's dad, and Shaggy himself. My low-grade

THE DARK DECEPTION

concern for him bloomed, expanding into an all-encompassing, full-body anxiety. I cracked my knuckles, frowning, while I concentrated on staring at the table. I couldn't face Shaggy's open, earnest eyes.

At a minimum, the Rogers family was about to face some serious scrutiny about their business affairs; at a maximum, Shaggy's dad was in serious trouble. Neither possibility was great, but one thing was for certain: The Rogers family had more secrets than all my old diaries combined.

Now it was up to us to discover them.

VELMA

SHAGGY WASN'T IN SCHOOL the next day. I shouldn't have been surprised—he was more likely to be found at the surfers' beach than stuck inside a classroom—but it didn't bode well for his state of mind. When he'd left my house last night, he'd seemed almost shell-shocked. Like everything he thought he knew about his dad was wrong.

I rubbed my eyes at my locker while I swapped out my chemistry book for the copy of *The Handmaid's Tale* we were reading in Contemporary Lit. I hadn't slept well, and I was feeling it. I'd kept waking up, first because I was so thirsty from that late-night pizza, and then, once I'd gulped a full glass of water, because I kept having dreams in which Mr. Rogers's face would appear on a crystal and float across my bedroom, calling my name.

THE DARK DECEPTION

"Still getting used to 'em, huh?"

I closed my locker door to find Fred Jones behind it. His blond head was ducked down, his shoulders sloped; it was almost like he was trying to shrink down into himself. He probably was, I realized; he probably didn't want anyone to see him talking to me. I didn't exactly do wonders for anyone's social status. Fred was subconsciously trying to hide, but, being Fred—tall, radiating energy—the attempt was futile.

I brushed aside the tingle I felt in my stomach and remembered Shaggy's party. The dance. Fred's arms around my waist. Aimee Drake's comment about how Shaggy had asked Fred to keep me away from him.

Suddenly, I wasn't tingly or tired at all. I was mad.

"What do you want, Fred?" I asked hotly. The warning bell had already rung, and the hallways were emptying.

"I was just saying hi," he said, his voice low.

I snorted. "Sure. Whatever you say."

"Hey." He looked wounded. "Did I . . . I mean, you okay?"

"I'm fantastic." I twirled my lock. "Right as rain. Peachy keen."

I didn't know why I was saying those things, or what I was trying to accomplish. But I couldn't seem to stop them from pouring out of my mouth. To my horror, more came.

"Good as gold. Hunky dory." Oh my god, I couldn't

stop. I watched Fred's face change from neutral to confused to concerned as cheesy clichés kept tumbling off my tongue.

"Um. Cool," he said. The final bell rang, and we stared at each other in anticipation. Would I continue spouting nonsense, or had my mouth finally caught up to my brain?

I fumbled for something else to say. The hallway was empty, and I was already officially late for class, so why not? "Did you want to talk more about my contacts?"

I don't know why, but what Fred did next made me even more angry: he smiled. He actually smiled, like he thought I was happy to see him, when really all I wanted to do was run away from him as fast as I could.

"Nah. I think I'm good."

And then Fred—Fred Jones, the guy who could (and did) get any girl he wanted, leaned over and tucked a stray strand of my hair behind my ear. "See ya," he whispered, and then spun on his heel and sauntered down the hallway.

I stood, still and silent, next to my locker for a few minutes. My heart was pounding so loudly I even turned around to check behind me a couple of times, to see if the sound was coming from someplace else.

But it was me. I was alone in the hallway, quiet on the outside and full of noise and chaos on the inside.

I channeled my confusion into solving the mystery of

THE DARK DECEPTION

the Crystal Cove Crystal, of the washed-up jewels, and of Shaggy. I had to; the pulsing energy Fred had left me with needed to go somewhere. And what better place than the most confusing case I'd ever worked on?

By lunchtime, I was ready to rip my hair out of my head. (Bonus: Doing so would probably confuse Fred Jones even more!) I stormed into the cafeteria and spotted my mark.

"We need to debrief," I said. Daphne was eating lunch—a salad this time—and when I approached her, her other friends—Aimee Drake and Shawna Foster and Haley Moriguchi—gave me a look and retreated to another table.

"I've been thinking the same thing all morning," Daphne said easily, pulling out her reporter's notebook. "French class was très ennuyeux, so I took the liberty of reassessing our suspect list."

I checked to make sure no one was looking at us too closely and read it eagerly:

> 1. **Samuel Rogers**—*motive (money), opportunity (it's his house!), no real alibi*

> 2. **Jack Rogers**—*motive (cash in on his family's wealth), opportunity (staying with the Rogerses), same alibi as Samuel Rogers*

3. **Taylor Burnett**—*no known motive (to help her mom? To fit in?), potential opportunity, alibi unknown*

4. **Noelle Burnett**—*no known motive, potential opportunity (no security in the Rogers house), alibi (working)*

5. **Milford Jones**—*motive (increased traffic on his website), potential opportunity, alibi unknown*

"Are these in order?" I wondered, hearing the doubt in my own voice. "Because if so, I'd swap some of these names. Milford, for one, belongs much higher."

Daphne groaned. "I know you hate him, V, but he can't have committed every crime Crystal Cove has ever seen. And remember how he came through for us when we rescued Marcy and the Hex Girls?"

"He's got all the motive in the world," I argued. "He's completely focused on crafting sensational stories to get views! And besides, even you can't deny he's shady."

She changed the subject. "What about Shaggy's dad?"

His always-pinched face flashed before my eyes. "Yep. Definitely at the top of the list."

"But is it too obvious?" Daphne furrowed her brow. Her

voice dropped. "Like, on paper he's the perfect villain. *Too perfect.*"

"The guy's got a lot to lose," I reminded her. "Desperation makes people do stupid things."

"What about Shaggy's mom, then? Shaggy knew a bit about his dad's finances, so I'm willing to bet Lieutenant Rogers knows even more. What lengths would she go to, to protect her family?"

I whistled. "Accusing the lieutenant is a risky move, Daph."

"I'm not accusing," she said, bristling. "I'm raising the idea."

"I mean, the entire Rogers family has a motive, right? Including Jack," I pointed out. "As far as we know, Shaggy's inheritance outranks his. Maybe he's concocted some grand scheme to become the rightful Rogers family heir? Even Shaggy sees the red flags. We need to find out more about him."

"Agreed. And then there's Noelle Burnett."

I scrunched up my face, thinking hard. "She's a liar, but what's her motive?"

"I can't figure her out." Daphne stared off into the distance for a moment. "She's mostly interested in getting Taylor to fit in, right? And getting people to shop in the jewelry store?"

"Yeah, and plus, she seems pretty tight with the

VELMA

Rogerses," I admitted. "Which brings us to . . ."

Daphne's finger hovered over Taylor's name. "I mean . . . she's just a kid."

"A kid who we might've seen lurking around the Haunted Village, leaving a clue behind. A kid who's always watching everyone. A kid whose mom lied to us," I put in.

"A kid who seems really lost," Daphne said.

I nodded. "Yeah. Lost is a good word for her."

We both stared at Daphne's notebook for a minute.

This was stupid, I realized. "We have to start at the beginning."

"Which beginning?" Daphne huffed. "We're all over the place here. I don't even know which lead to follow!"

"The jewels," I said. "They're the only real clue we have. We've got the ruby we found in the Haunted Village, but we need to get a good look at the rest. That'll help us figure out where they came from, which will lead us to a suspect." It had to. We were running out of options.

"Well, we already have one. But the rest are locked up in the police station," Daphne hissed, glancing around to make sure no one was listening. I followed her gaze and stopped when I noticed Taylor Burnett staring at us from the corner of the cafeteria. She stood alone, tray in hand, big brown eyes practically boring holes into us. "How exactly do you propose we get to them?"

I broke Taylor's stare. "*We* don't get to them. Shaggy does."

205

THE DARK DECEPTION

Daphne shook her head. "Shaggy's not even here. And he's not responding to any of my texts or calls."

"We can find him." I held up my phone. She peered at it and shot me a skeptical look.

"Why are you showing me Trey Moloney's social feed?"

"Look behind him." I pointed to the blurry figure behind Trey, who had, just ten minutes earlier, shared an image of his surfboard poking out of the sand down at the beach. His caption read, *Who needs lunch when the waves are this dope?*

I tucked my phone back in my pocket. "Ready?"

* * *

Sure, we lucked out, seeing Scooby in the background of Trey's photo, but it was no guarantee he and Shaggy would still be at the beach by the time we got there.

"Are we really cutting class to do this?" Daphne asked as we crossed the street, the beach mere feet away. The ocean leisurely tossed a few calm waves our way. Not much of a surf day, if you asked me.

"I signed into study hall and then snuck out when Mayer wasn't looking." I pointed at Daphne. Mr. Mayer was ancient and known for his lax rules about study hall sessions. "You, on the other hand, are definitely cutting class."

Daphne was more nervous than I'd seen her in a long time. Maybe ever. Or maybe it was a sign of too much caffeine. As we neared the beach, I noticed she kept cracking her knuckles—a sure sign she was anxious about something.

"Daph. What is it?" I finally asked. "You're worrying me."

"I . . ." She hesitated. A few clouds moved overhead, shading us in gray light. "Oh, look, there's Shaggy."

She pointed to the pack of surfers at the southern end of the beach. Shaggy's bright orange wetsuit emerged from the water. I blinked, goggled. That tall, muscular surfer was Shaggy?

"When did he turn into a male model?" I wondered aloud. Daphne ignored me.

We ran across the beach, sand flying. Halfway there, Scooby, noticing us, barked a hello, which made Shaggy notice us—and then noticeably shrink away.

"Oh no. Like, what now?" he moaned.

"Sorry," I said through gritted teeth. A couple of the other surfers—mostly older guys, though I did spot two college-aged girls paddling out—eyed us curiously. I shifted uncomfortably in the sand, kicking away a shell with my boot, and brushed away the hair stuck in my face after a gust of wind tousled it. My movement reminded me of Fred, and how he had done the same thing, and between that and the way these college guys were looking at me, I suddenly realized that all those years of being invisible were, quite possibly, preferable to being noticed like this. Couldn't a girl just talk to a friend on the beach without being ogled?

I was ready to let Daphne work her magic on Shaggy—partly because she was so good at it, and partly because I was having some serious second thoughts—but she was way off her game.

"So. Um. Velma and I were thinking . . ." She giggled uncharacteristically. "Well, Velma really thought it, not me. In fact, Velma, why don't you tell him?"

I stared at her in confusion. Who was this Daphne? I'd seen a lot of Daphne masks over the years—one for teachers, one for parents, one for Shawna and Aparna and Haley and that group, one for me—but I'd never seen nervous Daphne. Not like this.

Shaggy shook out some sand from his hair. "Like, can *someone* tell me?"

"Fine. Shaggy, we need to examine the jewels at the police station. We have one jewel we found . . . somewhere else." I took a deep breath, and then rushed on before he could ask about where we'd found the other jewel. "But we really need to see the rest of the evidence. And you're the only person who can get us what we need."

I held my breath as Shaggy processed this. It was one thing to run a shadow investigation like we were; it was entirely another to break the law while doing so. I couldn't believe we were doing this again. It was just a few weeks ago that the three of us—four, counting Scooby—had snuck into Shaggy's mom's office at the police station and logged into her computer to search for evidence. Back then, Shaggy had said we were "bending" the law—not breaking it. But stealing evidence was definitely more than just bending. I wondered if he would see it that way, too.

"Um . . . wow." He whistled and wiped a few droplets of water off his face. I noticed Daphne was looking at the water, the sand, the other surfers, the sky—anywhere but at Shaggy, here in his wetsuit. "You want to check out the jewels again, because you think there might be some kind of clue?"

"Maybe an identifying marker on them? Maybe something unique about their shape or size or color that can help us figure out where they came from?" I threw my hands up in the air. "I don't really know! Can you tell we're desperate?"

He nodded seriously. "Yeah, a little."

I snorted. "Thanks for your honesty. What do you think? Can you help us get into the evidence room?"

Shaggy stared out at the ocean for a few beats while I tried to breathe.

I tried again. "Shaggy . . . we're doing everything we can to get to the truth. And hopefully that truth will clear any misgivings you—or we—have about your dad. Please. Can you help us?"

He blinked as the waves crashed. Next to me, Daphne was practically vibrating. I couldn't take it anymore. I elbowed her. She jumped.

THE DARK DECEPTION

"Okay, fine!" Daphne cried, throwing her hands up in the air. "I give up! I'll tell you everything!"

Shaggy and I exchanged confused glances. "Huh?"

"I can't keep this secret anymore!" Daphne said.

"Keep . . . what secret?" I stuttered.

"But we have to go somewhere private first." She gestured to Shaggy's clothes in a pile on the sand. "Can you get dressed, please? Let's go to my house. I'll tell you everything. Better yet, I'll show you!"

I whispered to Shaggy, "I have no idea what she's talking about."

Within seconds, Shaggy had stripped off his wetsuit—he had swim shorts on underneath, but still, I turned away while he changed, because it just felt weird—and gotten back into his regular baggy shirt and jeans. I noticed Daphne was flushed, fanning herself against the mild, cool day.

"Come on." She practically ran off the beach, across Beach Street and up onto Maple Avenue toward her house. We struggled to keep up with her.

At last, we reached the Blake house—big and imposing like the Rogerses', and even more familiar to me than Shaggy's. Daphne unlocked the door and instructed us to sit at the dining room table. The house was dark and still; Daphne's dad was still on sabbatical in Tokyo, the twins were at school, and her mom and stepdad were at work.

VELMA

"Don't move," she warned us before disappearing.

Shaggy and I stared at each other while she was gone. After a few seconds of silence, my phone beeped with a text from an unknown number. I frowned at the screen. **Hey, is Shaggy with you?** it read.

I held up my screen to show him. He squinted at it and then relaxed back into his chair. "Tell her I'm fine."

"I'm not your secretary," I reminded him in disbelief. "Besides, I don't even know who it is!"

Shaggy exhaled just as his stomach rumbled. He pulled a candy bar out of his pocket. "It's Taylor. She knows I rarely check my phone."

"Well, you better start," I snapped. "And tell your little friend to lose my number. Texting someone you barely know like that is just plain weird."

Shaggy gaped at me, but I didn't care. Taylor was pressing all the wrong buttons—or, depending on whether her goal was to piss me off, all the right ones. And she seemed to be obsessed with Shaggy, which was . . . concerning. Not because Shaggy was a bad guy or anything, but because I worried the poor kid was going to get her heart broken.

Or maybe . . .

I thought about what we knew about Taylor so far while Shaggy played with the wrapper from his candy bar, and about what Daphne had said about her. She was a loner for sure and definitely socially awkward. (Hey, takes one to know one.) She gave off a vibe that was mostly unreadable but definitely landed in the "weird" zone. And, above all, she seemed to be semi-stalking Shaggy. That, combined with my suspicion that she'd been the one hanging around the Haunted Village, made me mentally move her to the top of the suspect list.

My phone dinged again. It was another text from the same number. Taylor.

I was just looking to see if he was home or not, it read, followed by the three little dots indicating she was still typing.

I waited for her next text, but it never came.

I wondered, was she desperate enough for his attention to steal something valuable to him . . . and pose as the Lady Vampire of the Bay?

DAPHNE

I RAN UP THE stairs and into my bedroom, my heart pounding. Once there, I quickly opened the bottom drawer of my desk and dug underneath the various old notebooks and term papers and childhood artwork I'd shoved in there until my hand hit what I was looking for: a box, its edges sharp and smooth.

Be cool, Daphne, I told myself as I carefully made my way back downstairs, holding the box like it contained the most fragile item in the world. And, in a way, it did.

Velma and Shaggy were right where I'd left them, except clearly Shaggy had raided the fridge in the two minutes I was gone, because he was halfway through the leftover veggie lasagna I'd wrapped up after dinner last night. Velma's eyes were wide, serious. Alarmed, even.

I set the box on the table and drew in a deep breath. This was going to be hard.

"I have a confession," I announced. My voice was shaky. I hadn't really planned this out, so I was winging it. I said the first thing that came to mind. "But first, some good news! We don't have to break in to the evidence room."

Shaggy breathed a sigh of relief and even Scooby, content, slumped to the hardwood floor with a satisfied *plop* and closed his eyes for a nap. Velma nodded, but then asked me the question I didn't want to answer, the question I'd been waiting for. "Why not?"

I tried to think about how to answer that. On the surface, it was a simple answer: We didn't need to break in to the police station to steal one of the washed-up jewels because we had one right here. I had one.

Yes, I'd kept one of the jewels from the beach.

It had been an accident at first. I hadn't noticed that one of them, a shiny emerald that matched my mother's green eyes perfectly, had caught on a thread in my pocket until I got home from the beach that night. I'd stared at it in my bedroom, flashing in the palm of my hand, and felt a sense of dread at the idea that I had to turn it in. That I had to part with it. And who would believe me, anyway? Daphne Blake liked jewelry, liked pretty clothes and material objects. That's what everyone thought. I couldn't face the possibility that someone might think I had stolen it. I couldn't bear to think of Ram reading about me in the police log.

But the real answer was more complicated.

My mom's birthday was just a few weeks away, and it was the first year since she'd left me—since the divorce when I'd forced her away, I reminded myself—that we were actually on good terms. On our way toward mending what we'd both broken. This year, I wanted something special for her, to show her how sorry I was and, more importantly, how seriously I took our relationship now. How much I wanted it to work. And so when I'd discovered the jewel in my pocket, I'd thought . . . well, what if this was the perfect gift? Elizabeth Blake had everything she could ever want— you'd be shocked at the amount of free stuff celebrities get!—and I'd thought, maybe a one-of-a-kind memento from Crystal Cove, the place that made her famous, would be just the thing.

It was stupid, I know. And unethical, and immoral, and a million other things. But when I saw the emerald, something sparked inside me. A greed. A hunger, almost. I wanted that jewel even though I knew I shouldn't keep it, *couldn't* keep it, because even after everything, I'm still that girl who is used to getting what she wants.

"Because," I finally said, opening the box, "we already have what we need."

We sat in silence at the dining room table, the

THE DARK DECEPTION

grandfather clock in the corner ticking away the minutes. Neither Velma nor Shaggy said a word. Even in the darkness (I hadn't turned on any lights, and the sky was growing more overcast by the second), the emerald shimmered.

"I can explain," I offered, my voice thick. "See, it was an accident. At first."

Velma held up a hand. "I need a minute here."

I nodded and listened to Scooby's light snoring. The shadows lengthened across the room. I glanced at Shaggy, who was staring in shock at the jewel, a heaping forkful of lasagna still in one hand.

Somewhere in the house, I heard a noise. But then Velma spoke.

"You've had this jewel in your possession all week?"

I forced a laugh. "Lucky break, right?"

"I mean . . . I guess?"

Shaggy finally made a move. He dropped his fork, pushed back his chair, and rushed over to me, looping his arms around my neck in a hug.

"Whoa," I said, nearly falling backward from the force of his hug. "What's that for?"

For a fraction of a second—I swear, just a fraction—I let myself relax into him, my body warming to his presence. Once I registered it, though, I kicked away the instinct and straightened up.

DAPHNE

"I really, really, really did not want to break in to the evidence room," he said into my hair. Then, like nothing had happened, he retreated to his seat and jammed the lasagna remains into his mouth.

"Okay," Velma said. "I guess it is a lucky break. I just wish . . ."

I met Velma's eyes. "I know."

"We're partners," she whispered, giving a half shrug like it was no big deal. But her eyes were bright and glassy, and her mouth was turned up in that way I knew meant she was holding something back.

"I should have told you right away," I agreed softly. "It won't happen again."

She nodded curtly. I felt my optimism collapse a little. I had promised myself a long time ago I'd make up for what I'd done to Velma when we were kids and everything fell apart, and now here was another thing I had to add to my apology list. I swallowed and tried to focus on what was next, but I vowed to do something nice—and wholly unexpected—for Velma at the next chance I could find. I already had an idea for what it might be.

"So." She inched her hand forward, toward the box, before pausing and casting a questioning glance my way. "May I?"

"Please."

She studied the jewel in silence, turning it over and

over again. She shone her phone's flashlight on it. It felt more like late evening than midafternoon, the way the room was cast in shadows, and we sat in the darkening gray light.

"I don't see anything notable about this jewel," she finally said. Then she pulled a wad of tissue paper from the pocket of her jeans, and unwrapped it to reveal the ruby we'd found in the Haunted Village. "And there's nothing special about this one, either." She laid it down next to the emerald.

Scooby's head popped up suddenly; he looked around and then lay back down and closed his eyes.

"Maybe we should take them both to Noelle?" Shaggy asked.

"Do we trust her?" I blurted.

"Or her daughter?" Velma mumbled.

Shaggy looked as surprised as I felt. "Like, why wouldn't you trust the Burnetts?"

I exchanged glances with Velma. She knew something, I could tell. "You first."

She shifted in her seat. "While you were upstairs, I started to wonder. Not about Noelle—we already know she's being kind of shady with us. But Taylor . . . well, she's kind of . . . clearly . . . like, seriously crushing on you, Shaggy."

Shaggy's eyebrows nearly leapt off his forehead. I wondered if mine were doing the same.

DAPHNE

Velma continued. "And I started to think about, when someone really wants to get someone else's attention, what extremes would they go to?" She drummed her fingers on the table.

"And?" I prompted.

Velma sighed. "And . . . she just texted me to ask if Shaggy was home or not."

It all started to click. Taylor wanted to make friends. And what better way was there to do that than to date one of the most popular guys in school? And what better way to snag that guy in school than to be there for him when he was going through tough times?

And the only way to do that was to *engineer* those "tough times."

"Oh my god," I said out loud. "Taylor stole the Crystal."

"And planted the jewels in the ocean, and the ruby in the Haunted Village," Velma concluded.

"What?!" Shaggy cried.

"She has the resources to do it, and the knowledge." Velma ticked off her fingers. "The motive, the opportunity, it's all there."

"I knew she was after something!" I said triumphantly.

"Like, I repeat, what?!" Shaggy said. "Taylor would never steal! And she is *not* crushing on me!"

The thought of Shaggy and Taylor being . . . well, *together* made me suddenly want to puke, so I pushed the vision away and tried to focus on what we knew.

"The other day, she even said something about . . ." Ack, I couldn't remember it exactly. I racked my brain. "Velma, you were there. Something about how this was a time to make things right in Crystal Cove. Remember?"

"Yes!" Velma jumped up and tucked her hair behind her ear. "At your party, Shaggy! She said, 'At least now we have a chance to help right some wrongs.'"

"You're wrong, Shaggy!" I cried, jabbing my finger in his chest harder than I intended. He recoiled, and I quickly corrected myself. "I mean, you're not wrong. That's not what I meant."

"What did you mean?" he asked, his voice small.

"I just mean, Taylor basically admitted she's here to fix something that went wrong. But what did she mean by that? Don't you think she could've meant the wrongs caused by the Vanishing? Your family is the only one who was left behind." I left out the part about how, right after she'd said that, she'd overheard Shawna and Nisha making fun of her. I deflated a little, realizing I could have tried a bit harder to smooth things over with her once I knew she'd heard them. Us.

My thoughts were interrupted by a scratching and unfamiliar sound that seemed to be coming from the second floor.

We all froze. "Did anyone else hear that?" I whispered.

They nodded. Scooby, now fully awake, stood at attention, his tail wagging.

A rush of wind slapped against the house, followed by the pitter-patter of rain on the windows. What I could see of the sky through the dining room windows was thick with gray clouds, darkening by the second.

Thud.

We all jumped in our seats.

Boom.

The hair on my arms was standing up, and in a flash I was, too, racing to the window. Lightning lit up the sky, cracking through the navy-blue clouds in bright orange streaks. The rain fell in sheets, and for a moment I thought I saw something in the backyard—near the pool, a blurry gray shape, moving fast.

I blinked, and all I could see was rain.

"Like, yikes," Shaggy whistled, still at the table.

Velma still held the emerald, turning it around in her hands and staring at it, lost in thought.

I flipped the light switch, so the room was flooded with light. There. That felt better. I returned to the table, trying to calm my racing heart—the lightning had surprised me, and between that and the adrenaline from confessing I had a jewel, my body felt loose, out of sorts. Drained.

And then, as I sat down, the lights flickered. With an audible click, we were swathed in darkness.

THE DARK DECEPTION

There was no use venturing out in the storm, so I made us some hot chocolate and brought the steaming mugs into the den, which was a shade brighter than the dining room and made me feel less alone somehow. Shaggy and Velma curled up on each end of the couch, so I took the love seat facing them.

"So is the power out everywhere, or just this neighborhood?" I asked Velma, who was checking her phone. She frowned.

"That's the weird thing. No one else seems to have been affected."

I shrugged and sipped my hot chocolate. Shaggy watched me, close enough that I began to grow uncomfortable. I wiped at my lip in case I had hot chocolate stuck on my face.

He scratched his craggy forehead. "I guess I'll just say it, then?"

"Say what, Shaggy?" Velma asked. Another round of lightning lit up the room, followed by a boom of thunder.

"Like, this whole thing just doesn't make any sense. Taylor's like a little sister to me! She has to know I'm not into her like that. And, like . . . why jewels? Like, specifically? Why not just break in to my house and steal the Crystal like a normal robber? And, like . . ." He rubbed the whiskers on his chin. "It just feels like nothing goes right here anymore."

"Like Crystal Cove is . . ." I prompted.

DAPHNE

"Cursed," Shaggy whispered.

Creak.

My heart leapt into my throat. Eyes wide, we stared at each other, somehow silently agreeing to remain still.

Creakkkkkkkk.

"The Vanished," Shaggy mouthed. I was somewhere between wanting to laugh or throw up, but Velma's face steered me closer to laughter.

"Don't be ridiculous," she whispered back. "Probably a—"

Stomp. Thud.

Scooby jumped into Shaggy's lap and whined.

"What do we do?" I hissed. I thought of the gray thing I'd seen by the pool, and the flash of red hair in the Haunted Village. The Lady Vampire of the Bay was known to haunt bodies of water, I remembered. What if it really was her? What if I'd somehow summoned her by keeping the jewel? What if—

"Hey, kids!"

I jumped out of my chair, my limbs shaking. I'd never been more relieved. "Mom! What are you doing here?"

My mother stood in the door of the room in fresh yoga pants and a sweatshirt, toweling off her wet hair.

"I live here. Well, temporarily. Remember?" she teased.

"We didn't know anyone was home." Velma's voice was small and tight.

"I was in the shower when the lights went out—I only

223

THE DARK DECEPTION

just heard your voices a few minutes ago." She sauntered over to the light switch on the wall and flicked it. The den was flooded with light again. "There you go. This house's electric has always been touchy during storms."

I swallowed and smoothed my hair, forcing myself to breathe as Scooby slid off Shaggy's lap. *Silly*, I told myself. *There was nothing by the pool. No ghosts. Not here!*

"Can I get you guys anything? What's that, hot chocolate? Nice!" My mother leaned in to smell the steam rising from my mug, pausing when she noticed the emerald and the ruby on the table. They sparkled under the bright lights she'd just turned on.

I thought fast. "Oh, just some jewels we're studying in chemistry."

My mother looked puzzled. "You're studying fake jewels in school?"

"They're real," Velma assured her.

My mother picked up the emerald, shot us all an amused look, and laughed out loud. "Who told you these were real?"

"Um . . ." I fumbled for words. What did she mean? Everyone said the jewels were real. Noelle had confirmed it. The *Howler* had reported it. The police believed it, and we had, too.

"Honey, I can tell real jewels from fake. And these are fake." She turned it over in her palm. "Good fakes! But definitely fake."

DAPHNE

"But Noelle said . . ." I protested. Velma rose from the couch and took the emerald and the ruby from my mother. Her lips were pursed; her cheeks red. She opened her mouth to speak, and I braced myself for the fire that would surely pour out of it.

Beep.

Ring.

Blip.

All at once, each of our phones dinged.

I pulled mine from my pocket, Velma grabbed hers from the table, and both Shaggy and my mother had theirs in their hands already.

Hands shaking, I studied my screen. I had a breaking news alert from the *Howler*. We all did:

They're Ba-ack! Town in Turmoil as More Mysterious Jewels Wash Ashore.

VELMA

DAPHNE'S MOTHER DIDN'T ASK questions; she just drove us downtown when we asked, pretending to ignore the heavy, forced silence filling the car. I'd never been more grateful for Daphne's rocky relationship with her mother; she'd clearly learned not to ask too many questions. Which was for the best, because we didn't have any answers.

But we knew someone who surely did.

"Taylor! Noelle!" I called as we burst into Burnett's. The storm had let up just enough so that I didn't feel like we were about to be blown into the ocean, but it was still raining. Raining hard enough that my hair was damp and my boots made squeaky noises on the shop's tiled floor.

Daphne, Shaggy, and Scooby were on my heels. Even before we looked in the back room, I could tell the place was empty. No one was here. The store just gave off that vibe—like someone had abandoned it in a hurry.

I could relate. Standing in Burnett's, thinking about how Noelle had told us nothing but lies, I'd expected to feel a low-grade rage simmering inside me. Instead I just felt hollow. Empty. I felt unmoored; adrift.

"Hello?" Daphne called futilely. She checked the front door again. "Why would Noelle leave this door unlocked?"

"We know you're here," I lied, my voice reverberating off the walls. "And we know you lied to us! The jewels are fake!"

Daphne circled behind the register, and I ducked under tables and peeked my head into the storage closet. Scooby sniffed around while Shaggy scratched his head and looked guilty. "I feel bad. Like, we shouldn't be in here without either of them," he said.

"Noelle's the one who should feel guilty," I snapped. "She told the world the jewels were real!" She told *me* the jewels were real, too, and I'd been cursing myself for my mistake ever since.

"They're definitely not here," Daphne said, wearily twisting her wet hair into a ponytail. "Which means . . ."

"Maybe they're down at the beach with the rest of Crystal Cove?" Shaggy suggested offhandedly, pointing out the window. People were streaming by, just like they had the first time the jewels had washed ashore. I narrowed

THE DARK DECEPTION

my eyes as I watched their heads bob by. Just like last time, everyone had received texts and calls and alerts that more jewels had appeared, that they should hurry to the beach to be part of the spectacle. For a moment déjà vu over-whelmed me. All this had happened already, and now it was happening again.

"Wait." I spun on my heels to face Daphne. "We know that the last time the jewels washed up, it was a diversion. Taylor needed the Rogers house empty in order to steal the Crystal."

Daphne stared at me for a beat, processing. Then she blanched. "Shaggy . . . where are your parents?"

He glanced at his phone. "My mom's at the beach, she just texted me. My dad's probably on his way, too." Then his eyes bulged. "My house. It's empty right now."

I met Daphne's eyes. We were both thinking the same thing.

"Shaggy, go!" I said.

Shaggy paused to glance at Daphne, who nodded. Then he and Scooby bolted for the door, running against the tide of people streaming toward the beach.

"What now?" Daphne asked.

"Now, we search for clues." I joined Daphne behind the register.

"Nothing out of the ordinary yet," she said, scanning the shelves under the counter. "Some paperwork—invoices, receipts, stuff like that. A few scraps of paper that have some weird names crossed out on them." She rifled through the random papers stacked around the old-fashioned register Noelle still had on the counter, although these days it was just for show—like the rest of Crystal Cove, Burnett's was a mix of retro charm and new technology—and then moved on to the small filing cabinet against the back wall.

To the side of the register was an open door, leading to a tiny storage room and office. There was a computer precariously positioned on the edge of a small table crowded with boxes, jewelry stands, and mannequin hands. "I'll take the storage room," I said.

I flipped on the light switch, wondering where to start. We had to get this right this time, and I felt the pressure pulling at my insides, twisting my stomach. We'd come this far, and now we needed proof. I refused to be made a fool of again, not when we were this close to answers.

I began digging through boxes, looking for something that would trigger that gut feeling I got whenever I was on the brink of solving a mystery. The hollowness inside me had morphed into something that felt, disappointingly, like shame; like embarrassment. It sat on my tongue like a bad spice. One of the reasons I hated the Detective Dinkley nickname Daphne had given me after our falling out was because it was meant to be diminishing. To make me feel *less* for wanting to solve mysteries. Because,

THE DARK DECEPTION

according to everyone else, a kid can't be a detective.

But I wasn't a kid anymore. I could solve mysteries, and I did. Together, with Daphne, we pieced together clues, filled in gaps, and found answers.

And that's why I couldn't stop blaming myself for not seeing this sooner. Noelle had lied to us from the beginning, even before any jewels had washed ashore or the Crystal had been stolen. Why hadn't I paid attention to that? Why hadn't I checked out Taylor a little more closely?

I knew why, I realized, turning over another box on the table in Noelle's office. I'd been distracted by something wholly unexpected and completely rattling.

And his name was Fred Jones.

"Anything?" Daphne asked.

"Not yet," I replied, trying to push the image of Fred's blond hair, his smile, out of my mind. I'd been distracted by Fred all week. I'd let myself think that maybe, possibly, there was more for me here in Crystal Cove than just being Detective Dinkley, resident freak. The kid who thought she was smarter than everybody else but who would never be taken seriously; who would always be looked through, talked over, shut out.

Well, I wouldn't make that mistake again.

Crunch.

My boot had hit something under the cramped table. I lifted it up.

VELMA

"Daph?" I said quietly.

"Mmm?"

"Come here."

"Just a sec. I'm almost done with this stack."

I didn't move. Even my foot, the one that had crushed the thing under the table, was still raised. I looked like a frozen flamingo.

"Why are you—Oh!"

Daphne rushed over and crouched down, shining her flashlight under the table. I dropped my foot, caught my balance, and joined her.

Bright red broken bits dotted the floor, like spatters of blood at a crime scene.

I reached out and fingered one of the pieces. It was sharp. "Glass," I breathed. Quickly, we gathered up all the bits—probably fifteen or so—and tried to piece them back together like a puzzle.

"Another ruby," Daphne murmured.

She was right. Pieced back together was a ruby. Or at least, what looked like a ruby. A fake one, made of glass that looked authentic. It was identical to the one we'd found in the Haunted Village.

"It's like your mom said," I told Daphne, regret thrumming in my throat. "It's a damn good fake."

DAPHNE

I WHIPPED OUT MY phone. "I'm calling the police."

"No." Velma held up a hand. "We don't have nearly enough evidence."

"It's the Burnetts!" I cried. "Or at least Taylor. It must've been her we saw in the Haunted Village! She left another ruby there to make us believe in the Lady Vampire. Think of all the ghost sightings this past week! It's Taylor! She's been dressing up and haunting the streets, just to cause chaos! And Noelle's covering up for her! One or both of them clearly planted those jewels. It all makes sense, Velma." My head spun as I ticked off the reasons one by one. "Taylor crafts a plan to get Shaggy's attention and to make her mother famous by being quoted in the media. Jeepers, don't you see? In fact, it's possible Milford is in on

232

DAPHNE

it, too! He gets legitimacy by interviewing a jewelry expert. Her business grows every time one of the *Howler's* posts about the Vanished or ghosts or whatever goes viral. And then Milford sells more papers. And Taylor gets the guy. Win-win-win."

"But why steal the Crystal?" Velma frowned.

I threw my hands up in the air. "Because it's worth a lot of money! Because they can pretend to 'find' it and start a whole new news cycle, starring themselves! The reasons are practically endless." I was so frustrated, so outraged, I wanted to throw something.

Velma nodded. "You're probably right, Daphne. But what do we do now? We still don't have proof. Some crushed costume jewelry on the floor of a jewelry shop? Your mom's word against the expert jeweler's? The police will just laugh at us. And I won't let that happen. Not again."

I paused, my thumb hovering over the Call button. I hated to admit it, but Velma was right. Two teenage girls trying to solve crimes? No one in Crystal Cove took us seriously. We knew that firsthand. We needed our case to be airtight.

While Velma watched, waiting for a response, I pulled up a new contact and tapped a few times. When I held my phone up to my ear, Velma's eyes widened.

"What are you doing?" she hissed.

"Getting proof."

Ram answered right away, his greeting soft and

welcoming, like he'd been waiting for me. It warmed me up inside. I didn't dare look at Velma. I knew she'd be making a face, a classic Velma expression that would make me feel like an idiot, even though I knew I was doing the smart thing. We needed help, and we were out of time. The ability to delegate well was one of my best assets, and I was going to use it.

"Blake!" His tone was teasing, light. For a moment I wanted to escape into it, into him, as if I could reach through our phones, over the Wi-Fi waves connecting us, and just . . . be. "What's up? Whose finances am I digging into this time?"

I laughed, feeling the heat of Velma's glare and ignoring it just the same. I glanced at the piece of scrap paper I was holding in my hand, the one from a little notebook next to the cash register. "Not finances this time. Plastics."

"Huh?"

"Here's the deal. The jewels were a diversion; the Crystal was always the target. In fact, we think the jewels are actually fake. And we're pretty sure we have a lead on the company that produced them."

"What?" Velma sidled up to me and snatched the paper from my hand. She'd been in the storage room when I'd first found it. I'd initially thought it was garbage; just a bunch of scribbled names that didn't make much sense. My eyes had skated over the letters without really registering

DAPHNE

them. But something about the note bothered me. It was the last name on the list, I realized a few minutes after I'd put it back on the counter and moved on to searching the cabinet, its letters dancing behind my eyelids. I knew that name: Purple Sea Plastics. One of Mr. Rogers' companies, its name an homage to the purple Crystal Cove Crystal.

"I'd call, but Velma and I need to get over to the Rogers house to make sure it's safe. And then we need to find Noelle and Taylor. Can you call some plastics factories nearby and see what they can find out? Like if a local jewelry shop has placed any large orders recently?"

Through the phone, Ram whistled. "The jewels are fake? Milford is going to be so, so pissed. Yeah, give me the names. I can call around right away."

I read him all the names, trying not to linger on the last one so as not to give him any hint that I had had a knee-jerk reaction to seeing a Rogers-owned brand on the list.

"As fast as you can," I reminded him, thinking of Shaggy rushing to the Rogers house to protect it. Of the Burnetts, who were gone.

"You got it, boss," he teased.

I lit up like a firework inside. It felt like now or never, like I needed to make a gesture of some kind to let him know where my head was at. I'd never asked out a guy before; they usually came to me. But Ram seemed to like it when I bossed him around.

THE DARK DECEPTION

It was time to take the leap. To jump, and see if he would catch me.

"And . . . Ram?"

"Yeah?"

My heart danced wildly in my chest. I ducked my head so Velma wouldn't see my face flushed from hope, from embarrassment. "When this is all over, maybe we can . . . maybe we can see a movie or something?"

The line was quiet. The store was quiet. All I could hear was my heart throbbing and Velma's quick breaths as she stood across from me, staring at me. I closed my eyes. *Please, Ram*, I wanted to add. *Don't leave me hanging like this. Not now.*

"That sounds like a great idea, Blake." *Click.*

I opened my eyes and took a deep breath. I almost laughed—Ram said yes! We were going on a proper date!—when I saw Velma and regained my cool. I cleared my throat.

"So, what now?" I asked.

"Now we find the Burnetts." She sighed, a half smile curling up the side of her face. "And hopefully your lover boy finds some answers."

I smiled. "He will." I'd never been so sure of anything.

* * *

Once again, I'd worn the wrong shoes for a ghost hunt. My boots pounded against the sidewalk as Velma and I jogged through the streets. The rain had stopped. As we ran, our

236

DAPHNE

feet kicked up splashes of puddles and debris, little twigs and leaves climbing up our legs. Velma dialed Shaggy and put him on speakerphone.

"Like, it's all clear!" he said when he finally picked up. His voice was breathless, but it might've just been the speakerphone. "Nothing's missing! I'm gonna head to the beach and see what's up there."

"Make sure you lock up and set the alarm before you leave!" Velma said.

"Like, you got it, V," he said.

No sooner had we hung up with Shaggy on Velma's phone than my phone rang, Ram's name flashing across the screen. I answered it, realizing as I did that, with Shaggy's intel, we no longer needed to hit up the Rogers place. Velma and I reversed course, taking a sharp turn back toward the beach. We really needed a vehicle, but I'd left my car at home. I briefly fantasized about reusing that old van we used as Mystery Inc. headquarters when we were kids.

"What's the word?" I asked Ram.

"I got it," he declared. I flipped Velma a thumbs-up and tapped the Speaker button as my heart soared. "Purple Sea Plastics confirmed they sold two separate shipments of a thousand fake gemstones over the past three weeks to a business in the town of Crystal Cove, though they refused to name the company, citing client confidentiality."

"Yes!" I high-fived Velma. "Thanks, Ram. I owe you big-time."

"Yep," he said with a smile in his voice. "But there's more."

"Oh yeah? What is it?" I asked.

"The police scanner just reported a suspicious figure at the Rogers place. I'm gonna head over there and see what I can find."

We frowned at each other. "Shaggy just told us he's home and everything's fine."

"Well, it sounded like they were taking it seriously. I figure enough reporters are down at the beach, so I'll take the house and see if anything happens."

"Okay. Let's connect on this in a bit, then?"

"Sure. Oh, wait. I almost forgot." I heard Ram flip through his notebook, the pages rustling over the phone. "Not sure if this helps you or not, but the guy I talked to at Purple Sea couldn't confirm there was a Noelle or a Taylor involved at all. He says a man placed the order. Someone named Jack, no last name. Does that ring a bell?"

I felt my jaw loosen and drop. I met Velma's eyes; her face held the same shocked expression as mine.

After a moment I realized Ram was waiting for a response. "Um, cool, thanks. Bye." I hurriedly hung up.

We were mere blocks from the beach and in the far-off distance I could hear the hum of a crowd, the

DAPHNE

undercurrent of buzzing about whatever new jewels had washed ashore. Velma and I stared at each other. We'd come so far on this case, only to end up back at Jack. Shaggy's mysterious cousin, who as far as we could tell had no reason at all to be placing an order for fake gemstones under the Burnetts' orders.

"There are tons of people named Jack." Velma broke the silence. Her face belied a skepticism her tone was hiding.

"I can think of a dozen off the top of my head," I agreed.

Still, we stood, unmoving, as the weight of the storm lingered in the air around us. My throat was tight, my stomach curdling. After a moment I realized what was setting my teeth on edge. "It will ruin Shaggy if his favorite cousin is somehow involved in this."

Velma paused before nodding. Maybe, like me, she was afraid to talk. Like saying it out loud would make it true.

I allowed myself one minute, a single collection of sixty seconds, to worry about my friend. Shaggy, who only wanted good things in the world; who could never get his family to see him the way the rest of us did.

And then I exhaled, stiffened my spine, smoothed my hair, and grabbed Velma's hand. "We should get to the beach."

"Not the beach," Velma said tightly. And it was

something about the way she said it just then; it all clicked into place for me. Crystal Cove locals know about the way the tide pulls at the sea caves; how a kid's toy bucket that's dropped on one end of the caves winds up on the other side of the beach a few hours later. Those tides, that current, as predictable as the sunrise, as the weekend special at the diner.

It would be easy, I realized. Simple, really. For someone—a local—to pinpoint almost exactly where they needed to "drop" a bunch of items into the water on the north side of the caves in order to have them wash up on in a precise spot at the opposite end of the beach. To make the town gather, paving the way for a robbery that was so bold, so symbolic, it could shake Crystal Cove to its core.

"The sea caves."

The rain has let up, but the air is still heavy and thick with salt, with shame. She carries it with her, too. She always has. Her whole family has borne its weight for far too long.

Now they will be free of it. Now things will be as they should.

As she walks deeper, deeper than most have ever ventured, the sea caves slope upward and the sound of rushing waves heightens. How thick are these walls? she wonders. She reaches out to touch one—it is slimy, warm. She thinks she can hear it speak to her.

"Come," it whispers. "Farther."

She follows instructions well. Her arms ache. The Crystal is heavy now and growing warmer by the second. Its faint glow is the only light in the caves, and if she squints just the right way, she can believe it is guiding her forward, pointing a ray to the path it wants her to take.

Up, back, more. Beyond. The sea caves are endless. There is always another tunnel that breaks off into a few more, always another way forward.

She hears an unmistakable hiss: "Here."

Her arms release the Crystal. She unwraps it carefully, lovingly. How honored is she to be the one who gets to do this. To right this wrong. How grateful her people will be.

"Are you sure?"

The unexpected voice makes her nearly drop the Crystal. That wouldn't do. She tsks and ignores the question.

It is far too late for questions now.

Once unwrapped, she places the Crystal on the floor of the cave and pats some sand around it. To protect it. To welcome it home.

As if it understands, the ground heaves, as if breathing a sigh of relief.

VELMA

THE THING ABOUT THE sea caves was, they were nearly endless. While many of them had been mapped and explored, there were way too many—little offshoots from the main caves, dark mouths that yawned open and then curled back onto themselves—and it was easy to get lost. I couldn't believe we were back here so soon after the *last* mystery Crystal Cove had had to face.

On the other side of the caves, most of Crystal Cove's residents appeared to be gathering. We could hear murmurs of their conversations as they floated on the tidal air, ricocheting off the craggy landscape, sounding both so close and so far away.

"They could be anywhere in here." The worry in my voice echoed at the mouth of the main cave. Daphne and

I stood, ankle deep in the water, having shed our boots on the sand. We'd texted Shaggy to come meet us.

The last time we'd been here, we'd found a bunch of missing girls held hostage deep inside. This time, we were looking for something less sinister . . . but, in a way, more confusing. It was enough to make you believe there was something about Crystal Cove, something in the water, that made people lose themselves, all in the name of lore, of legends and ghosts and magic. Would we ever *not* bear the stain of the Vanished?

Staring into the abyss, I worried I already knew the answer.

"Come on," I said heavily, kicking through the foaming water. "They're probably not too far in, since they need to be close to the water to dump the jewels."

"Stay close," Daphne instructed. I nodded and gripped her hand. We were in agreement there.

We'd barely taken three steps into the mouth of the cave when we heard a bark and a series of splashes.

"Scooby!" I could hear the relief in Daphne's voice. Scooby, tail wagging, leapt through the water as he splashed toward us. Shaggy's long legs appeared behind him.

"We can help," Shaggy said. "Scooby knows the Burnetts pretty well. Scooby, go!"

At his command, Scooby took off, and we rushed to follow him. The next cave split off into four openings, and Scooby darted for the third one from the right.

"Like, let's go!" Shaggy panted. We picked up speed. Behind us, the late afternoon light was quickly fading. It was getting hard to see.

I was about to ask Daphne if we should call the police when we heard a shout, a bark, and a cry, in that order.

"Taylor!" Shaggy yelled, taking off. The light was disappearing rapidly, and within seconds Shaggy was swallowed up by the darkness. The caves sloped upward in this section, and we trudged after him, our feet thick with damp sand. My legs burned.

"Over here!"

I heard Shaggy before I saw him, and then, a burst of light. Daphne had turned on her phone's flashlight and it caught on a pile of sparkles, casting hundreds of tiny lights over the cave's walls and ceiling. It was . . . beautiful.

It was also *proof.*

"Hey!" I cried, running over to where Shaggy stood. Scooby was sniffing around, pacing between the cave's walls, as Shaggy stared and pointed at the source of the light: two large boxes, multicolored jewels leaking out of them. And in between, fury painted on their matching faces, were Noelle and Taylor. "Gotcha!"

"Drop it, Taylor!" Daphne shouted.

"Huh?" Taylor brushed her bangs out of her eyes and

245

eyed us in surprise. "What are you guys doing here? How did you . . ."

"We know what you're up to," Daphne said accusingly. "We figured it all out."

"You don't get it!" Noelle spat. In the dim light, her face was cast in long shadows. Her anger was palpable; I could practically feel it heating up the walls, the sand. "I had to do it!"

"Oh, we get it," Daphne said. "Your daughter here orchestrated this whole thing, just to impress Shaggy. How cliché."

"What?" Noelle asked blankly.

"No," Taylor whispered. She looked shocked to see us, but there was something else underneath the surprise. I studied her face and realized: It was shame.

Daphne, unfazed, barked out a sarcastic laugh. "We know Taylor roped you into this crazy scheme!"

But Noelle was shaking her head, protesting, and something about the way she said no made me think, for the first time, she was telling the truth.

"Listen, I get it," I said suddenly. I stepped forward, enclosing myself into a little circle with just me, Noelle, Taylor, and the jewels. I swallowed, my mind racing, my voice low and intimate. "I get what it's like to not fit in. It can make a girl pretty . . . well, desperate sometimes. But it gets better. I promise, Taylor. It does."

I heard a sniffle behind me. Daphne, I knew, thinking about that day when, at ten years old, my whole world collapsed around me: my parents' jobs, our house, our friendship. Everything, gone seemingly overnight, and things were never the same after that.

"Your sob story is irrelevant," Noelle sneered. I stepped back. A sliver of fear cut through my stomach at the expression in her eyes. "You have no idea what you're talking about. Yes, you caught me. I dumped the jewels. I lied. And I took the Crystal Cove Crystal. But I had a right to. It's mine!"

I heard a gasp from Daphne, a whine from Scooby. I glanced at Shaggy. He was staring at Noelle, silent, his pale skin almost translucent in the glittering light.

"What?" he whispered.

Noelle lunged at him, jabbing a finger into his face. Scooby leapt to attention, placing himself in between Noelle and Shaggy. He growled.

Taylor grabbed her mother's elbow. "Mom, please, stop," she begged.

But Noelle was rolling now, letting loose with her long-held litany of complaints. "The Burnetts have been in Crystal Cove almost as long as the Rogerses. But we get no respect! The Rogerses have stolen everything from this town! I had to get back what's rightfully ours! Taylor has nothing to do with this!"

Her movements were stilted, tight. Robotic, almost. It was like she wanted to hold in these thoughts and feelings that had been building up inside her for so long, but she just couldn't do it anymore, and she spat them out in a pitch that was much higher than her usual speaking voice. Like she couldn't control her own voice.

"But I thought..." Daphne's voice trailed off. She flicked her eyes between Taylor and Noelle, and then her expression cleared. "Oh."

"You didn't know?" I said to Taylor. Her scared eyes darted toward her mother before landing back on me. She shook her head nervously, like she didn't want to.

She was torn, Taylor. Anyone could see that.

And suddenly, I saw what she really was, what we should have seen all along: not a creepy new girl who was crushing on and stalking one of my oldest friends. She was just a scared kid dealing with some problems she couldn't control. Whose mom had put her up to some weird stunts that she'd probably explained as practical jokes. But there was nothing funny about what Noelle was really up to.

Shaggy's voice was flat, his face emotionless, as he processed Noelle's admission. "You ... stole the Crystal?"

"Stole it?" Noelle howled. For a moment it felt like I was back in the haunted amusement park where I'd worked, with the canned recording of screaming voices blaring through the hidden speakers in the haunted house ride. "I didn't *steal* it. I took it back. It doesn't belong to you, it belongs to us all," she hissed. "The Rogerses can't keep getting away with your lies, your *deceptions*. I'll show everyone who you really are!"

"Mom!" Taylor was openly crying now, gripping her mother's arm. Tugging at it. But Noelle didn't seem to notice. "Just come with me, please! Stop this!"

Just behind Shaggy's eyes, there was a crumpling. A flash of pain before his face settled back into its usual placid, blank expression. "But you've known my family . . . like, forever."

"Yes, forever, and we still never got an invitation to your house," Noelle raged, her eyes like lightning. "Every party your parents threw, every fund-raiser, we'd wait for our invitation. Your mother, your grandmother, your great-grandmother would come into the store and pore over necklaces and bracelets with my parents and me before making their selections for what jewels to flaunt at whatever gala they were hosting. But we never got an invitation to the ball. Our families go back generations, yet we were never good enough to associate with you publicly!"

Noelle's eyes bulged. Her breath was ragged, echoing through the cave, through our shocked silence. She flailed her arms as she spoke, and the movements were jerky; something about her body's awkward gesticulations triggered a new level of panic inside me. Noelle wasn't just mad, I realized. She was dangerous.

And then I saw it, glinting in the light from Daphne's phone. I froze. It was almost like my body registered the danger before my eyes could. *Run*, my legs told me.

But I forced myself to stay. To look.

It was a knife.

Sleek and silver and long, it waved back and forth in Noelle's hand in triumph. A sick, satisfied smile stretched across her face as she grabbed Shaggy with her free hand and pulled him close to her. Close to the knife's shining blade.

As if by instinct, Daphne stepped toward him. "No!" she cried. Scooby growled at Noelle.

But Noelle just pulled Shaggy closer to her, lifting the blade to his throat. He shook his head at Daphne and me, a warning in his eyes. I swallowed. I knew he'd do anything to protect us—and Scooby and Taylor.

"And when I moved away, for years I had to listen to my parents' complaints and worries as the Rogerses used them. Ignored them!" Noelle ranted. "They grew older and weaker, and still the Rogers family couldn't be bothered. The two oldest families in Crystal Cove, but we were never good enough for you. You Rogerses are all the same— greedy and selfish and small. Do you know, when my parents died, your parents didn't even send flowers?"

Taylor was whispering now, begging. "Put it down, Mom. Give it to me. Please. Don't hurt Shaggy. He's our friend, I swear."

I had a sick feeling in my stomach, a swirling, like a tornado was circling my insides. I had to do something. Keeping my hand close to my body, leveraging the way Noelle seemed to be distracted, focusing all her ire on Shaggy, I tapped a frantic text message to the first person I could think of.

911, send police to the caves! I wrote. The *whoosh* of the Send button was barely audible over the roar of Noelle, over the sobs of Taylor, over the steady thrum of the tide flowing in and out of the cave.

I began to wonder what was more dangerous: the rising tide, or Noelle herself.

But then she moved the knife around again, brandishing it closer to Shaggy's neck. The tide was beyond my control, I decided, but Noelle was not. Not yet, anyway.

She wasn't finished. "My parents just wanted some acknowledgment for all the ways they've supported the Rogers family over the years," she hissed. "If someone had given them that, they might still be here with us."

Shaggy stood in front of her, still as a statue and just as silent. She was irate, spouting horrible accusations about how Shaggy's parents had helped speed up her own parents' deaths. About how no one in Crystal Cove treated her family well enough, no one respected their legacy. About the Rogers family's deception, their duplicity.

"That isn't true, Mom, stop it," Taylor said. "You said

THE DARK DECEPTION

you wanted to come back here to make things right with our neighbors. But not like this! Stop it, Mom! Please!"

But Noelle didn't seem to hear Taylor. "You've never let anyone in this town forget that you were the first ones here. Like it matters. This place is cursed!" Her eyes dimmed; her face crumpled. "And my daughter . . . you promised, Shaggy. You promised she'd belong here."

I swallowed, cleared my throat. Behind me Daphne murmured a warning. She could tell I was about to interrupt, and she didn't want me to.

But did I have a choice? We had to keep Noelle busy, distracted from the fact that she had a weapon in her hands and every reason—in her mind—to use it.

"Everyone feels the same way about my family," I said quietly. Surprised, Noelle looked my way. The knife faltered, moved a few inches away from Shaggy's exposed Adam's apple; I pretended not to notice. "My mom's not from Crystal Cove. Her family's not even from America. And some people . . . well, they never let her forget that. They think it makes her inferior somehow."

"That's what I'm saying!" Noelle exclaimed. "No one here ever lets you forget where you came from! We Burnetts were the first to settle here after the Vanishing, but, noooo, since we aren't descended from the original settlers, Samuel Rogers thinks we don't count. And I'm sick of it! And of them!"

252

"But—" Shaggy began to protest. He tried to step forward, away from her.

It was the wrong move. Noelle jerked him closer, bringing the knife's edge right up against the flesh of his throat. I choked back a scream.

"Shut up," Noelle commanded. "I will never forgive the Rogers family."

She let that declaration hang in the air. I stared at the knife, my mind racing with ideas and yet also, somehow, paralyzed with fear. I couldn't move. The whole thing felt like a scene in a play, and one wrong move could make the theater explode.

And then Taylor, tiny and meek, stepped closer to her mother.

My stomach dropped.

But Taylor's voice rang out across the darkness of the caves, stronger and surer than I'd ever heard it. "Mother," she said sharply, holding out a hand. "This is too much. I love you, but we're done here."

Noelle blinked. She turned and stared at her daughter.

Drip, drip, whoosh, went the water. I heard my own heartbeat racing in my ears; I felt it thrumming in my lungs.

"I loved your parents, Noelle," Shaggy said, his voice thick with the threat of tears. "And Taylor is like a sister to me. I'm so sorry you think that . . . like, that my family . . ." He couldn't get the words out.

THE DARK DECEPTION

"You're just as bad as your father," Noelle countered, turning away from Taylor. Her arm was still raised, the knife close to his heart now. "What's worse is, you don't even know it."

"I'm sorry if you think that's true," he said quietly. "But I . . ."

"This isn't about you," Noelle spat. "This is about your father. He'll get what's coming to him, believe me!"

Shaggy swallowed hard. "Please, Noelle. Don't."

"Mom," Taylor begged.

Noelle pulled Shaggy closer.

"Please," Taylor whispered. "Mommy. Put it down. For me."

A sob broke out of Noelle, her body convulsing.

"Freeze!"

The voice boomed, a long, lingering note that seemed to come from the cave walls. We halted, each of us, and I felt my bones loosen in relief as a trio of flashlights rounded the corner of the cave, casting a spotlight over our terrified tableau. Noelle blinked in surprise, and then screamed.

Lieutenant Rogers appeared first, running up the sand with one hand on her flashlight and the other on her holster. Behind her were two deputies, who immediately surrounded Noelle. She collapsed to her knees and raised her hands in the air. When one of the officer's flashlights landed on her face; she looked defeated. The burn from her eyes had dissipated, replaced with a blank stare.

As soon as Noelle was safely in cuffs, Lieutenant Rogers turned to Shaggy. "All right?" she asked. Her voice sounded curt, but I could see the concern in her eyes.

So could Shaggy, who nodded. "Where's the Crystal?" he asked, his voice high, scared.

"Where it belongs." Noelle fixed Lieutenant Rogers with a stare. One of the deputies began reading Noelle her rights. "That Crystal is from these caves, and that's where it will stay."

"You just left it out here? Like, unprotected?" Shaggy was aghast.

Noelle's face darkened as Lieutenant Rogers pulled her to her feet, her wrists locked tightly in front of her. "It's where it has to be. The Rogerses have never understood that."

"Come on," Shaggy's mother said, gesturing for the other two officers to lead her out of the caves. "You too," she added, nodding to Taylor.

Taylor crossed her arms, her eyes cast to the ground, her long brown hair doing its best to hide her, to cover her.

As they rounded the corner, Noelle's voice rang out once more. "It has to remain here in the caves! Only then will the curse on this town finally be lifted! Only then will all this deception end!"

THE DARK DECEPTION

* * *

We stood in silence for a few minutes, me and Daphne and Shaggy, and even Scooby, who had decided it was the perfect time to take a nap. He was curled up near Shaggy's feet, eyes closed.

Noelle's final words still rang in my ears, almost as if the walls of the cave were refusing to let them go. My heart clenched as I repeated them to myself. *Only then will the curse on this town be lifted.*

"Hey," Daphne said softly. Shaggy shook his head, as if waking himself from a trance, and looked at her. "You okay?"

He stared for a moment. Anyone could see he was not, in fact, okay. His skin was still paler than usual; his eyes glassy.

"Like, see?" he finally said, low and tense. I strained to hear him. "This is why Scooby and I keep to ourselves. Nobody wants a Rogers around. We're poison. Just like this whole place."

Suddenly, footsteps. A throat clearing. At the entrance of the cave, backed by the dull reflection of flashing police lights, stood two tall, slim silhouettes. One figure stepped forward, out of the shadows and into the ray of light from Daphne's phone.

"Come, son." Mr. Rogers beckoned. Behind him, Jack Rogers stood, a mirror image of his uncle.

If they had heard what Shaggy had just said, they didn't let on. As always, Mr. Rogers's face was unreadable, his presence commanding. I was used to being invisible, but the way he looked only at Shaggy was a new sensation, even for me. It wasn't that he didn't see me or Daphne; it was that it didn't matter whether he did or didn't. *We* didn't matter.

Without a word or a look back, Shaggy heeded his family's call. Scooby roused himself from his nap and followed, leaving Daphne and me alone in the glittering dark.

DAPHNE

I BLINKED FURIOUSLY WHEN we finally made our way out of the sea caves and back into the fresh air. The sky was still gray, but it was one of those bright grays—like a blank canvas, waiting for a fresh coat of paint. I breathed in the air, embraced the cool water circling my feet.

Velma and I treaded carefully toward the beach. Rocks jutted out from the sand at all angles and heights, and I forged a path through them using the breaking sea foam as my guide. Up ahead, past the sand, several police cars blocked the road, sirens off but lights flashing, like someone had muted the chase scene of a movie. I felt dazed, like I'd just awoken from a bad dream, an unexpected nap.

We found our shoes and brushed the wet sand from our feet as best we could, neither of us saying anything.

DAPHNE

What was there to say right now? Later, we'd need to discuss what Noelle had said about the curse of Crystal Cove, and what to do with poor Taylor. I couldn't believe what her mom had put her up to. Posing as the Lady Vampire, following me and Velma around to throw us off the case . . . it was something no teenager should have to deal with.

But all that, we'd have to deal with later. Right now? Now I just wanted something warm to drink, and maybe someone warm to drink it with.

A text bleated at me. It was Ram, saying he had to tell me something. Warmth pooled inside me, and I responded with a thumbs-up. Later, I'd check in with him, but first, I needed to change out of my wet clothes and wash my rained-on hair. My body was damp from the caves, my limbs hollowed out from the rush and then retreat of adrenaline.

We crossed Beach Street and cut through the crowds of Crystal Cove residents pouring toward the mouth of the caves, staring at the woman in handcuffs being escorted into a police car. I scanned the crowd for Shaggy, but neither he nor his father were anywhere to be seen.

Velma followed me home—my house was closer— where we waved hello to my little sisters and my stepdad (I avoided him when he asked us if we'd seen the mess down at the beach) and then collapsed in my bedroom. I was almost too tired to shower, but then I realized I wanted

THE DARK DECEPTION

to pop into the *Howler* offices and see what the latest article was shaping up to be. And, of course, see if Ram was there.

After my shower I found Velma sitting at my desk chair, phone in her hand and an unreadable expression on her face. "Daph?" she said hesitantly when she saw me.

"Taking a hot shower after solving a mystery is really the perfect method of self-care," I said as I combed my hair. "You wanna hop in?"

Velma didn't say anything, just continued looking at me with a weird mixture of fear and apprehension on her face. She looked, I realized, like the sky was about to fall, and she had to be the one to break the news.

"V, what is it?" I started to get that seed of worry in my stomach. It danced around, threatening to bloom.

"Um . . ." She stalled, glancing at her phone and then back at me, her eyes wide. I dropped my brush and rushed over to the desk, where my own phone was charging. A breaking news alert from the *Howler* flashed back at me.

The Kids Are All Right! Local Intern a Hero after Solving Spate of Local Mysteries.

For a second, I wondered who the headline was referring to. And then I realized . . . it had to be me.

Milford must have heard all about how Velma and I had solved the case, about how we figured out the jewels were a diversion and the Crystal was the real get; about how we'd chased Noelle into the caves and tracked down the factory she'd used—and he'd been so impressed with me, his lowly intern, that he'd written a profile all about me.

And then I read the damn thing.

* * *

It was pretty late when I arrived at the *Howler* offices, and the office park was near deserted. While most people had long gone home, I knew Ram would be there; he'd posted a video to his social feed. I wasn't sure I'd ever forget the image: him sitting at the desk next to mine, looking directly into the camera and raising a glass of sparkling cider. He'd linked to the *Howler*'s headline in his caption. Already, his post had two hundred likes.

Velma escorted me all the way to the elevators on the ground floor. Her tirade had begun in my bedroom and still hadn't let up. I had a headache forming behind my eyes and a flame of anger cresting through my veins. It was almost comforting, to be in that spot again—anger had always been what I'd done best, had always been my refuge. My rage was a weapon I'd long ago learned how to wield.

"This is unbelievable!" she fumed. "He's trying to take all the credit for our hard work! How on earth can he justify this to himself? Throughout history men have been doing this exact same thing. Look at all the famous men who ignored or dismissed the contributions their female partners made! From scientific breakthroughs to art to novels to computers—ugh, it just makes me so mad! Aren't you mad, Daphne?!"

Mad didn't cover it. I was *pissed*. But I'd also learned some things about myself recently, and in that moment, standing with Velma—who had enough anger for the both of us—I decided to look deeper. To look inward.

And underneath my anger I found . . . disappointment. Grief, even.

I, Daphne Blake, was sad.

I held up a hand weakly, my throat aching. "Yes. Please. Just stop. I know."

"But it's unacceptable! He thinks just because he's a man, he can steal this story from you? I—"

"Velma," I said more firmly, pressing the Up button. "Enough. I got this."

We heard the elevator whooshing through its shaft, and I saw the change in Velma's face, the way her muscles relaxed, like all the air had been let out of her. I nearly smiled then. Velma's fury was different than mine, but it came from the right place. She had my back, and I'd never been more grateful.

"You got this," she repeated. I nodded. And when the elevator dinged and the door opened, I stepped in, leaving her behind. I had to do this on my own.

I stepped off the elevator and into what can only be described as a full-fledged party, of which Ram was the star. Milford and the other *Howler* executives and staff were in the large conference room, drinking from the many opened bottles of champagne that lined the table. A tower of empty pizza boxes sat under the windows; music was playing from someone's computer but, with all the celebratory conversations, I couldn't make out what it was.

It didn't matter. My eyes landed on Ram, who was seated at the head of the conference room table, wearing a smile so wide I could practically see his molars.

Seeing him, I realized I'd already burned through all my anger on the way over here. Now I was just . . . disappointed.

It was as if my disappointment formed tentacles, became a living, breathing thing of its own, and reached out through the glass walls of the conference room to slither into Ram's lap, because just then, he looked right at me. And his smile faltered.

Ram hesitated for a moment before standing up, shaking a few hands, getting a few pats on his back in that way guys do to each other, and then slipping through the door, his eyes darting over to me. Without a word I escaped through the stairwell, taking the steps two at a time until I reached the top-floor cafeteria. I assumed it would be empty at this time of evening, and it was; even the ever-present coffeepots had been flicked off, the rising moon reflecting off their dregs.

I stood at the wall of windows overlooking Crystal

Cove. I'd never noticed it before, but from here I could see the roof of my own house as well as the faint outline of the Dinkley property. Downtown, the lights flickered on—the movie theater marquee, the charming lamps dotting every street corner—and as I watched them, the oddest sensation washed over me. It was like I'd slipped on an invisible hazmat suit, closing me off from the rest of the world. I even felt it on my face—a tightening of my jaw, an unconscious gritting of my teeth. It was a shutting in of sorts—a click of a lever, a lock sliding into place. By the time Ram appeared at the windows next to me, my transformation was complete. I had shut myself down completely, and there was no way in or out.

"Blake." Ram's voice was apologetic, cutting through the silence of the cafeteria. He panted a little, out of breath from the stairs. His desperation was palpable; thin and stringy, like I could pluck it from him in strands. "I can explain."

I couldn't tear my eyes away from the lights downtown, at the way I could see people, small and fast, scurrying through the streets. The day's thunderstorm had opened up the sky, pushed the haze and clouds away, leaving us with a clear, star-filled night. I imagined I could hear the noises of downtown—the clinking of dishes in the diner, the buzzing of the popcorn machine at the theater, the grinding of beans at The Mocha. I wondered how many of the people enjoying the night down there were still thinking of the jewels, or the Crystal. Of Noelle, of the Vanished, of the ghosts that haunted us.

A lump formed in my throat. It was strange how you could be in a building full of people, standing next to one in particular you had spent a lot of time thinking about, and still feel so alone.

"Please, Blake. It wasn't my idea," Ram tried again. And it was the wheedling tone that did it for me, that cracked open the armor just enough for some of my emotions to spill out. I couldn't stop them.

I slowly faced him. "Tell me, Ram. How's it feel to be a hero?"

His jaw twitched. His dark eyes glinted. "I'm not a hero."

My face contorted into a smirk. "No kidding."

"I didn't ask for that headline."

"But I bet you didn't fight it, either," I said flatly. My voice didn't sound like my own. It was robotic. My body was, too; all creaky elbows and tightened muscles. I'd never felt less like myself.

"What was I supposed to do?" Ram pulled at his hair. "Milford knew I was working on this story and demanded to see what I had. I updated him just as we got confirmation there'd been an arrest. And . . ."

He raised his hands, shrugged. As if that were enough

to convince me, to make me understand that he'd had no control over the outcome, no voice in how the story should be told. Or by whom.

"I trusted you," I said slowly, realizing in that moment how big a deal that had been. How new it had felt for me, how scary and exciting at the same time—to crack myself open the tiniest of bits and let in some light. "I even convinced *Velma* to trust you."

"You *can* trust me!"

I barked out a bitter laugh and crossed my arms over my chest. The moonlight shifted; someone downstairs turned up the music, and the bass pounded through the floor. The party was still going strong. A celebration of the *Howler*'s coverage of events, of Ram's quick thinking.

"Sure, Ram," I said. "You've really convinced me of that with this stunt."

Ram pulled at his hair again, his face twisting. "You don't understand. I'm not like you, Blake. I don't have your connections. Your famous mom, your lawyer dad. I had to fight like crazy to make it this far."

"Ah." I nodded as if I understood, even agreed. "So it's my own fault, then, for being a Blake. Cool."

"No! It's not! I'm just saying! To help you understand! I've been here a full year, toiling away, and then you waltzed in and had all these great ideas. And Milford loved you right away!" He sighed, paused. Met my eyes. Something in

DAPHNE

them softened; his voice dropped. "The truth is, I was jealous, Blake. You have everything you could ever want. You're . . . fantastic. But you have to believe me—I didn't plan any of this. Honestly. It all just spun out of control."

I stared at him in awe. It was wild how someone could be so into someone else—could be daydreaming about a future, about a relationship—and then have it so utterly turned upside down in a single moment, or by a single headline.

Something new burst forward in me then, warm and thick. With a jolt I realized what it was: embarrassment. What a fool I'd been, thinking I could reveal my true self to someone. My cheeks warmed at my mistake.

"You know . . ." I stammered, feeling out the words. "I really liked you, Ram."

"You can still like me!" he exclaimed. "Please, Blake."

I shook my head, eyes trained on the floor. I couldn't even answer him; my throat was locked up, my lips glued shut.

"I get that you're mad. And you have every right to be. But I have to tell you something, something related to the case." Ram's tone had shifted. He was all business now, but earnest, like he really needed me to hear this.

"Tell it to Milford."

"No, seriously. It's about Jack."

Jack was the furthest thing from my mind in that moment. I shook my head. "I don't care."

"If I know anything about you, Daphne Blake, it's that you want the truth. The whole story." Ram hesitated. When I didn't interject, he continued. "I don't know what it means, if it means anything at all. But you should know . . . when I got to the Rogers mansion, Jack Rogers was there. At least, I assume it was Jack Rogers. He looked like an older version of your friend Shaggy."

"So?" I was tired; uninterested, even. It had been the longest of days.

"So . . . he didn't see me, Blake." Ram's eyes bored into mine, like there was a secret message in them I was supposed to decipher. But I was done trying to figure Ram out; the only person I needed to figure out was myself. "He was carting boxes out of the garage and into his car. And he was doing it in a hurry. He looked manic. Scared, even. And I . . . well, I guess I just wanted you to know. Because of your relationship with Shaggy."

My mouth dropped open, but Ram just shrugged. "He seems like he's a good friend of yours, I mean."

Right. Friends. Yes, Shaggy and I were friends.

"So . . ." Ram drew out the word. I let him. I let it linger over us.

Finally, I said, "So is that it, then? That's what you wanted to tell me?"

Ram opened his mouth, closed it, opened it again.

We stayed still, silent, for so long that the motion-sensor

lights in the cafeteria flicked off, swathing us in darkness. We stayed there, moonlight cutting across the room, until I decided I could control my body enough to walk away, that I was strong enough for the physical act of moving. I'd forgotten how much it ached, keeping this wall around me.

But not as much as it had hurt to let someone in only to have them attack from the inside.

DAPHNE AND VELMA

DAPHNE

AFTER A DAY OF searching, and with help from Taylor, the police found the Crystal Cove Crystal half-buried in one of the deepest sea caves, about a quarter mile behind where we'd found Noelle. While that cave appeared to be above sea level, a not-uncommon mix of high tides and a storm surge could've easily crept up one night and washed it out into the deep ocean. And none of us would have ever known.

It really made me wonder about other things the ocean has taken from those caves over the years. And what it's left behind.

I was deep in thought the next day at school, and Velma was noticeably worried about me. She kept casting

DAPHNE AND VELMA

nervous glances at me every time we passed each other in the halls.

Finally, when we sat down to lunch, I snapped at her. "Stop looking at me so much! You're creeping me out!"

"I'm just trying to gauge where you're at today," she said nervously. She pushed her hair behind her ears and leaned in. "This isn't like you, Daph. Even your other friends are concerned."

Velma surreptitiously pointed at a nearby table, where Haley Moriguchi and Shawna Foster and Aimee Drake were sitting. I glanced at them and, sure enough, they were staring at me. Quickly they looked away and all pretended to be super interested in their lunches. Which, having purchased one myself—a bland salad with barely edible grilled chicken and two lonely slices of cucumber—was highly unlikely.

I sighed. "I'll deal with them later. They can't handle moody Daphne."

Velma made a sympathetic face. "Funny, because moody Daphne is the only Daphne I *can* handle."

I smiled despite myself. Velma took the opportunity to try to lift my spirits.

"Listen, some good things happened this week! It wasn't a total bust. We solved the mystery of the gems!"

"But not the mystery we set out to solve," I muttered as Shaggy jogged past us, a sandwich in each hand. He never

271

even looked our way. Watching him disappear through the lunch crowd, I wondered whether he really meant what he'd said, about being poison.

Because the thing was, I felt a little like that, too. Like maybe the real stuff inside me, the true Daphne, was so toxic, so opposite of what people wanted me to be, that I could never reveal it to anyone. Look what had happened when I'd tried.

I tore my eyes away from Shaggy and noticed Velma hesitating. "What?" I asked her. "Spill it."

"I do have a question for you," she admitted. Her eyebrows twisted into a straight line. "You trust me, right?"

Surprised, I nodded. "Of course."

She looked at her hands. "It's just . . . there were a few times this week where it seemed like you didn't. Like you were more interested in what . . . someone else had to say about things."

"You mean Ram," I realized, bristling.

She nodded, shrugged. "It just felt like . . . I don't know. We're supposed to be partners. And sometimes it didn't feel like we were."

I stared at the table. There was a tightness in my chest, like I was zipping in my feelings again. "Don't worry," I assured her. "That won't happen again."

I didn't tell her about the surprise I had planned for her, but I hoped it would show her how sorry I was.

VELMA

I DRAGGED MYSELF HOME, my backpack heavy on my shoulders, kicking at the leaves cluttering the sidewalks. It was Friday afternoon and, for the first time in a week, it felt like, finally, no one in Crystal Cove was talking about ghosts. Even the *Howler* had moved on; the day's headlines were all about some controversy brewing over a local business ordinance that was coming up for a vote.

Taylor hadn't been back to school, but I tracked down Shaggy and he said he'd spoken to her and said she seemed as okay as she could be. It turned out her mom had talked her into helping with some of the ghost sightings that had happened around town, including the stunt Daphne had witnessed in the Haunted Village. But Shaggy said she didn't really understand what her mom had been up to—she'd thought it was all an elaborate prank—and I believed her.

Noelle had tapped into the town's fears so easily. She understood the power of suggestion, just like Frank had said. Half the incidents people had reported were innocuous, but their importance had become inflated in their own minds, and why? Because of fear. Daphne and I had felt it, even in our own homes.

The power of suggestion was strong . . . so strong that Noelle had used it on the spur of the moment with the Lady

THE DARK DECEPTION

Vampire of the Bay. She'd heard that Mr. Rogers had mentioned the Lady Vampire at the beach when the jewels had been discovered. All she'd had to do to our overactive imaginations was walk the shoreline in a red wig and a long, flowing cloak. And Taylor had been her unwitting accomplice.

All that was over now, but I still felt bad for Taylor. All she'd wanted was to find a place where she belonged. She'd believed it was here, but after everything her mom had put the town through, it wouldn't be easy. Daphne and I had plans to reach out to her when the dust had settled a bit more.

So, all told, I was grateful for the calm and quiet that had returned to my life. But it didn't last long.

"Boo!"

I jumped when a figure popped out of the bushes in front of me. Fred Jones laughed when he saw the look on my face.

"Zoinks, Fred," I complained, gripping at my chest. But who can say, really, whether my heart was racing from the scare, or from his presence?

He was still laughing. I rolled my eyes and stepped around him. I just wanted to go home.

"No, wait!" he called after me.

"What is it, Fred?" I heard the impatience in my voice, even though I was trying to keep it cool, even.

He shrugged and fell into step next to me, his shoulder bumping into mine. "Just saying hey."

I shot him a sideways look. It was a mistake, that look, because he was especially striking from that angle.

A stalk of bravery shot up inside me. *Now or never*, I realized. "I owe you a thanks," I said. "For calling the police the other day."

"No problem," Fred said easily. Then again, Fred said *everything* easily. His whole life was easiness, simplicity, lighthearted fun.

"Well, you really helped me out with that," I added. Then I paused before bringing up what I really wanted to tell him. "We're even now, okay? You don't have to keep following me around." I stared straight ahead, concentrating on moving my feet forward.

"Huh?"

"I know Shaggy asked you to keep me occupied so I would stop tracking him." I paused for emphasis, facing him on the sidewalk. "But the case is closed. I'm not following Shaggy anymore, so you don't have to follow me."

Fred's wide face was blank. He stared at me, not moving a muscle.

"Don't you get it, Fred?" I tried again, simpler this time. "You're released from whatever promise you gave to Shaggy. You don't have to keep me occupied anymore. I'll leave Shaggy alone."

Fred whistled lowly, smoothed a strand of his blond hair back from his forehead. "Dinkley, I have no idea what you're talking about."

I shifted impatiently. "At Shaggy's party. When he asked you to keep an eye on me so I wouldn't bother him. I know all about it, it's fine."

But Fred shook his head. "Shaggy never asked me that."

I stared at him, frozen. I'd overheard Aimee Drake and Aparna Din saying that, hadn't I?

And I'd believed them. Because of course Fred Jones wouldn't have asked me to dance if he hadn't been instructed to by one of his oldest friends. I mean . . . right?

Our staring contest lengthened until, finally, Fred shrugged again. His whole face changed when he smiled— his blue eyes crinkled; his sharp jaw softened and rounded.

"Anyway," he said. "Have a good weekend."

And then he waved, darted into the street, and broke into a jog, disappearing across someone's bright green lawn.

I was so lost in thought the rest of the way home that, somehow, I ended up at our new-old house rather than the apartment. Well, it was my favorite place to think, anyway, so I crossed the lawn, unlocked the back door, and stepped inside. I could think of no better way to spend the end of a long week than hanging out, alone, in the house that was helping put my family back together again.

DAPHNE AND VELMA

But when I stepped inside, I nearly fell over.

My hands shook as I grabbed my phone and dialed. When Daphne answered, I could barely choke out the words. "We have a new mystery! Someone's broken into our new house and . . . and . . . well . . . cleaned it!"

The house was spotless—cleared of the leaves and other debris the wind had dragged in, free of the dust and grime we hadn't gotten around to cleaning yet. It shone.

But Daphne just laughed. "Consider it a housewarming present."

"What? You did this?" I sputtered.

"No!" Daphne sounded horrified. "But I hired an agency. My stepdad still feels bad about how long it took to get the house back in your dad's name. This was actually his idea! And I feel bad about . . . well, I just wanted to do something special for you. Your family's been through a lot."

Wow. "So has yours," I reminded her, hearing a crack in my voice. Quickly I cleared my throat. "Thanks."

When we hung up, I had something in my eyes. (Okay, fine. It was tears. I had tears in my eyes.) I rubbed and then winced—I kept forgetting how to operate these stupid contacts.

I popped into the bathroom, marveling at the pure white porcelain sink (it had previously been a dull off-white), and stared in the mirror.

I saw me, but incomplete. I blinked and rubbed my eyes again.

I'd been carrying my old glasses around in my backpack all week, just in case I'd had a problem with my new contacts. Well, here was the problem, I finally realized: I didn't like them. I didn't *want* to get used to them. My little experiment was over.

Squinting, I popped out the little lenses and grabbed my glasses. They slipped on like a glove. Satisfied, I pushed them up the bridge of my nose and grinned at my reflection.

"Ah," I said, nodding. Fred's face flashed before me and I paused, wondering what he was going to say when he saw me at school on Monday.

Then I realized: It didn't matter. I didn't care. I was Velma Dinkley, and I wore glasses and solved mysteries and loved my cat and had one of the greatest best friends the world had ever known.

And I was perfectly happy, for maybe the first time I could ever remember, to be me.

DAPHNE

I COULDN'T BELIEVE MY eyes when the name flashed up on my screen. I rubbed them, brushing away the dream I'd been in the middle of, and checked again.

What was Shaggy doing calling me at seven in the

morning? Actually, scratch that: What was Shaggy doing calling me at all?

"Hello?" I mumbled, trying to find my voice in the morning fog.

"Daph?"

He sounded far away.

He sounded scared.

I sat up in bed and flung off my blankets. "Shaggy? What's up?"

"It's happened."

Something in his voice . . . it made me ice cold. I burrowed back under my blankets. "What happened? What do you mean?"

When he didn't answer, I said, "You're scaring me, Shaggy."

"It's, like, all over," he finally said. "Check the papers."

He hung up.

I threw myself out of bed and ran to my desk, opening up my laptop. I checked a bunch of news sites—the *Howler* but also the national networks.

Shaggy was right. It was everywhere.

Rogers Enterprises in Financial Ruin; CEO Samuel Rogers Faces Charges of Fraud, Embezzlement, Extortion.

I went down the rabbit hole, parsing through story after story, until I found what I somehow knew I would find.

What I'd been looking for since the moment I'd heard Shaggy's voice.

The first story to report on Rogers Enterprises, the breaking news that was referenced and quoted in every other article in mainstream media, came from a familiar name. A young reporter, just starting out.

Ramsay Hansen.

ABOUT THE AUTHOR

Morgan Baden's debut young adult novel, *The Hive*, cowritten with her husband Barry Lyga, was named a Best Book of Fall 2019 by *People* magazine and was called "a gripping, tense, action-packed thriller" by *Booklist*. An established and bestselling ghost writer, Morgan is also a communications consultant who has led social media and internal communications for iconic children's book brands. She lives in New Jersey with her husband and two children.